Eamon Kelly was born in Kerry. His first job as an actor was with the Radio Éireann Repertory Company where he spent twelve years. He was two years with the Gate Theatre. He played in the long Broadway run of Brial Friel's *Philadelphia, Here I Come!* and for the part of the father in the play he received a Tony Award nomination for the best Supporting Actor and Variety's poll of the New York Critics Award for the same role in 1966-7. He has been with the Abbey since 1967.

Eamon Kelly's storytelling evenings have brought him to many corners of America and England. His other books include *In My Father's Time, Bless Me Father, The Rub of a Relic* and *According to Custom.*

D0840708

English that for me
and
Your humble servant

Two Nights of Storytelling

Eamon Kelly

THE MERCIER PRESS

THE MERCIER PRESS, 4 Bridge Street, Cork
24 Lower Abbey Street, Dublin 1

© Eamon Kelly, 1990
ISBN 0 85342 936 7

English that for me was written for the stage by Eamon Kelly and first presented at the Peacock Theatre on 30 June 1980. It was directed by Michael Colgan.

Your humble servant was written for the stage by Eamon Kelly and first presented by The Abbey Theatre at the Peacock Theatre on 17 August 1983. It was directed by Raymond Yeates.

This book is sold subject to the condition that it shall not, by way of trade or otherwise, be lent, re-sold, hired out, or otherwise circulated without the publisher's prior consent. This book is copyright, and it is an infringement of copyright to reproduce this book, in whole or in part, by any process whatsoever. The material may not be performed without a licence. Applications for same must be made in advance to:
THE MERCIER PRESS,
4 Bridge Street, Cork.

The characters and situations in this book are entirely imaginary and bear no relation to any real person or actual happening. Any resemblance to real persons, living or dead, is purely conincidental.

Printed by Litho Press Co., Midleton, Co. Cork.

Contents

YOUR HUMBLE SERVANT

ENGLISH THAT FOR ME

Introduction

When W. B. Yeats, the Nobel Prize author and poet founded the Abbey Theatre he coupled the new stage with the folk narrative tradition in Ireland. When he and Lady Gregory were not engaged on working or writing for the theatre, they went out in the countryside to listen to storytelling.

The person who knew his material thoroughly and could hold his listeners spellbound with his narration was called 'seanchaí' in Irish (or as we call it, Gaelic), and he was a man of importance. He lives again in the Abbey Theatre. He is called Eamon Kelly, and he combines the primitive delight of storytelling with distinguished artistry. His type is rare, at least outside of Ireland. He has a big name here. His one-man show has drawn full houses all the summer in the Abbey's Peacock.

Although Kelly himself uses properties and gestures in a minimal way (he sits in a kitchen set-piece, at the table, with a fire on the hearth with the teapot warming) he seems to let speech pour through him, and to become his story. One is captivated by this and even if one misses the point of some Gaelic expression, one savours the beauty of the English language in itself, when it is spoken as Eamon Kelly speaks it.*

Paradoxically, perhaps, as in so much else here, the English language is improved by its contact with Irish, or, rather refreshed by sea wind and drifting clouds. Certainly it is as if the speech drives from outside into Eamon Kelly's cosy room.

The exposition also has to do with language form. 'English that for me' and already in the grammatical construction, using 'English' as a verb, we see this relationship between Irish and English and the reciprocal meaning it has for Irish people and for their consciousness of themselves.

Eamon Kelly has a living connection with the land and its tradition, he comes from a line of craftsmen in Killarney, and was himself a carpenter before he became an amateur actor. Here is another vital element in the development of the Irish theatre, nearness to a popular amateur tradition in a country poor in theatres.

A one-man show built upon a folk foundation and with a certain play upon priests and Catholic religiosity, turns our thoughts to the Italian actor and author Dario Fo. But the difference between the two is at the same time clear. When Fo improvises, Kelly plans his effects with care; where Fo is bitingly sarcastic, Kelly is genially ironic. On the whole, with Fo in mind, one is struck with how Kelly is so unaggressive in dealing with material which is so thunderously political, for instance, the Irish language or the power of the Church. But the connection between art and politics, between language and history is inevitably more complex than we at home would gladly imagine during the last decade. But we can see it here.

Erik Pierstorff
Oslo Dagbladet

*See glossary for translations

1
The King of the Lies

The three sure things that show a man is falling into old age are: one, a fondness for money, two, forgetfulness . . . and I forget now what the third one is! Oh, yes, itchiness.

Where I slept last night
There was commotion there.
With ducks and geese
And a gander there.
The yella drop down
It fell on my crown,
And I slept ne'r a wink
With the fleas, my boy.

They've no fleas now in Sweden! A Professor there is mad looking to lay his hands on a few. He wants them for some experiment. But who'll admit they have them? No one! A Gortnabrochus woman said to a Raynasup woman one day, 'You'll always know those with fleas. Fleas always follow people with big mouths!' And the Raynasup woman making her mouth into a little roundy 'O' said, 'Is that so!'

The first fine day in spring, my grandmother'd carry the bed clothes out in the yard and spread them abroad on the hedge, and there she'd be belting the feather tick with the stave of a barrel, and dust flying out of it! This day a tramp was passing and seeing her flaking the tick, 'The right way to get rid of 'em!' says he.

My grandmother was mortified. A very respectable woman, one of the Buckley's of Glounacoppel that always wore a dandy cap. To think that she'd have the like! So the tramp seeing her blushing said, 'You needn't be one sign ashamed, Ma'am, the queen of England have 'em!'

It was said Queen Victoria was peppering in dread of fleas, so she must know they were there. When she visited Killarney in 1884, Lord Kenmare's gamekeeper had to sit on his grug* outside her room door, at the ready in case of an attack! The Killarney fleas were outrageous. They could hop as high as the cathedral and bred with such rapidity that every little crab-jaw of them coming into the world was a grandfather inside of twenty-four hours.

The Swedish Professor'd be in his element that time for the world was full of fleas. Two hundred years ago Dublin had a very vicious brand of them. They came in in the turf from the Bog of Allen. Oh, they were a terror altogether. Worse than the flying fleas of Italy that bit Peter Shea to death on his way home from Rome after getting forgiveness for striking his father! A man told me that the Dublin fleas were the cause of the Act of Union, for the members of the Old Irish Parliament, who were a bit classy in themselves, refused to sit in the chamber, for he said they couldn't sit in the chamber, always on the move, so no motion could be carried. 'Twas worse than the entertainment house in Cork they used to call 'Lourdes', because if you went in a cripple you came out 'walking'!

A fox one time was 'walking', so what did he do? He put a ball of wool in his mouth and sunk his tail into the lake. Bit by bit, ever so gradual so as not to create a panic. Then as it became dampish and uncomfortable for them, the passengers moved up in the bus. And the fox, taking his time, let his tailboard into the lake, diaidh ar ndiaidh síos le fánaigh* until the water was up to his ears, and when he was full sure and certain the fleas had collected into the wool in his mouth he let the ball go and diving down he said, 'If that ship'll sink it won't be for the want of a crew!'

My uncle's father-in-law, a mine of information, told me he was one day out fowling. A muzzle loader he had.

'And after tamping down the powder,' he said, 'I forgot to take the ramrod out of it! I fired at a batch of geese, and they must be flying one over the other in formation, for the ramrod went up through three of 'em. They fell down and spiked a salmon that was rising for a fly — the surprise he got! I waded into the river and when I was backing out with my three geese and my salmon, damnit if I didn't trip and fall down on a hare that was passing and killed him!'

That is if you could believe him!

There was a king one time in the eastern world and he had no family only one daughter, as fine a girl as ever looked out on air or land. The king himself was falling into years and the way he'd like to pass the time was listening to stories — the bigger the lie, the better he liked it, and the nick-name for him was, 'The King of the Lies'! In time he got tired of his own storytellers as the lies they told him brought him no comfort, so he let it be known far and wide that he would give his daughter in marriage and half of his kingdom to any young man that could tell him a story so outlandish and tell it so well that it would make the king forget himself and say, 'You're a liar. That never happened!'

At that time there was a widow woman living in Ireland and she had a son whose name was Timmy. A fine boy! If he had any fault at all it was that he was a liar, but a gracious liar for he spoke like a bishop. Timmy heard of the king's pronouncement so he said to his mother, 'I suppose I'll have to get married sometime so I might as well marry where money is. Throw a few things together for me I'm going on a journey.'

So she washed his shirt, baked a cake and killed a cock and he hit the road a welt* for the eastern world, and going up he knocked at the door, and the king came out.

'What brought you?' the king said.

'My two legs,' says Timmy, 'that won't take me to the grave!'

'Come on away in,' the king said, and he put Timmy sitting that way by the side of the fire and the king sat here. The king's wife was there at the table preparing the dinner and the king said to her, 'There should be a couple o' bottles of stout below there in the room. Throw us up a one!'

She brought up two. The king took the caps off them, and handed one to Timmy. They had a few slugs out of them, and looking then towards the table where the wife was working, the king said, 'I'll bet you anything now you never saw turnips as big as them in all your life before!'

'I didn't too,' says Timmy, 'my mother had turnips sat in Páirc na bPoll last year and do you know how big they were? Well, we had a young sow, she was a while back after being with the gentleman, and she went astray. High up or low down, we couldn't find her. What was it, you diggle,* but she broke into the garden and ate her way into a turnip and that turnip was so enormous that she had a litter of banbhs* inside in it. The banbhs* were six weeks old and fit for the market before she tunnelled her way out the other side!'

The king finished the bottle of stout and put it on the hob.

'Come on away out here!' he said. And he brought Timmy out in the haggard. 'I'll bet you now,' says he, 'you never saw so many bee-hives in the one place before!'

'I didn't so,' says Timmy, 'we have a hive for every day in the year. And it is my job to stand at the gate of the haggard every morning and count the bees going out, and be there again in the evening to count 'em coming home in case any one of 'em'd be dodging the column. One evening I was a bee short! I went looking for her, and made off the hill behind the house where I had a good view of the countryside. There was a horse there and I jumped on his back, that lifted me another few feet, and looking around me what should I see away over from me at the edge of

Merry's Wood but my bee. I galloped down on the horse and there was the bee so full of honey that she couldn't lift a wing.

'With my penknife, I cut a whole lot of sally rods to make two baskets — you know like sráthar fhadas* — and filled 'em up with honey, not a bad day's work for a bee! When I loaded the honey on to the horse, a big hollow came in his back from the weight, and when I clapped the bee down between the two baskets, if the horse's back didn't break! I caught a long spar that was there and I said to the horse, 'Open your mouth!' and I ran the spar back through him and out behind to reinforce the backbone. I took him by the head then and brought him up to the house. We had so much honey that year we were giving it to the pigs!'

'Come on away down here,' says the king and he opened the gate into the orchard and looked at a lofty cherry tree, you'd know he was very proud of it. 'I'll bet you now,' says the king, 'you never saw a tree as tall as that before.'

'I didn't so,' says Timmy. 'There's a cherry tree growing in my mother's orchard at home with branches reaching up into the clouds, and that tree is so tall isn't it up through the middle of it I go to heaven to Mass every Sunday for we're living a bit away for the chapel. Well, I was this Sunday above in heaven and a storm broke and knocked the cherry tree. Wasn't that a nice pucker to be in. When I was walking around heaven after the breakfast in the morning I saw three women winnowing oats and I said to myself, 'Wherever there's grain, there's straw'. I got a couple of loads of it, and began to make a súgán* rope and as I twisted it I added to it and let it fall down from me until I thought it was long enough to go to the ground, then I hitched my own end of it to the gate of heaven and down with me hand under hand. Well the view I had, and everything went fine until the súgán* broke and looking down, I saw that I had another good mile to go before I'd settle. With great presence of mind, I took an apple out of my pocket and threw it down our chimney. My mother ran out opening her apron and I fell into it, but whatever rotten material was in the apron, I went down through it like a pillaloo* through a country, rolled over and fell into the river and sank to the bottom of the pool. When I opened my eyes, there was this big laverick* of a salmon passing. I put my hands around him and waltzed him out on the bank. I brought him in home and throwing him that way on the table, I said to my mother, 'We'll have a bit of him for the dinner.' She opened the salmon and what fell out of his belly but this big book. And there printed in the very first page, was that your father worked for my father for one and fourpence a day with his shoes off on soft ground shaving gooseberries!'

'You're a liar,' says the king, 'that never happened!'

'That's the daughter gone now!' says Timmy.

Timmy married the daughter and got half of the kingdom, and when he came home here on holidays after, he was so rich, a pound note he'd light the pipe with!

2
My Uncle's Father-in-law's Father

My uncle's father-in-law's father claimed that he was the first man to put English on *Rí na mBreag* — The King of the Lies! For when he was small Irish is all that was in the world. He said the only place you'd hear English was in the chapel on Sunday. At that time, same as now, a goodly proportion of the men used to be outside the chapel door. It didn't make any difference how much room there was inside in the body of the church, outside they'd be, all down on one knee praying away. And I remember one Sunday some unchristian blackguard hopped a pebble off Ger Balbh's* bald plate.

'May God look down on me!' Ger bellowed in Irish. 'Who did that?'

Ger's shout, so out of place at the church door, gave rise to a burst of hilarity from some of the men. On hearing the commotion the parish priest that was just about to go out on the altar to read the acts of faith, hope and charity came out of the sacristy. But his footsteps on the gravel gave his approach away, and when he arrived at the front door the men were calm and devout. All kneeling up straight except Ger Balbh*.

'Did I hear voices raised in anger at the door of God's house?' the parish priest asked.

No answer, but a murmur of fervent prayer. Then seeing Ger Balbh* with his right elbow on his right knee and his left knee on his cap on the ground, he said to him, 'Go down on your other knee.'

Ger changed from his left to his right knee.

'Go down on you other knee,' the parish priest said again. Ger changed back — as he was at first.

'Go down on your two knees,' the parish priest ordered.

'Blessed God!' says Ger. 'A wonder you didn't say that at first, father!'

But as soon as the sermon'd start, such was the interest in English at the time, that the men'd crowd into the bottom of the chapel, moving forward and sideways so as to be in a good position to drink in the sermon, as a man said to me, 'not so much for the sin as the syntax'.

You got a dig that time from the man near you if you coughed. 'Éist,'* he'd say, in case he'd miss any word. And there were men and such were their powers of retention that they'd bring the entire sermon with them and that night you'd find them standing up on a kitchen chair giving out the sermon again to a crowded kitchen, so the people used to have reams of it off. For it was vented out on them that English was the coming thing and that they'd get no place without it!

But my uncle's father-in-law's father said to me that the bulk of the congregation at that time didn't know no more than a crow what the priest was saying — standing there with their mouths open, but they loved the sound of it. The women moreover. The women used to marvel at the grand stream of speech flowing out of Father Bolger, and the lovely accent he had, and the way he used to say, 'Constantinoble'.

He didn't make half as good a job of Gort-na-Bro-chus — and it was nearer to him! Or Macantsamhraidh, when he was calling out the stations. Like the pebbles rolling on the sea shore, a lot of the awkwardness was knocked off those place-names so that strangers coming into the locality could get their tongues around them. Some place-names were changed altogether. Look at the attempt that was made to make Little's Fort out of Lissivigeen, a name so sweet that it is always at the end of the robin's song. The local people, backed by whatever priest was in Killarney at the time, resisted that change. But people elsewhere didn't have the same spirit and *Árd na Gamhna*, where the poet Eagán was born, became Calfmount, and *Cnuicín na hEórnan* became Cornhill. And it wasn't alone place-names that were changed. When they were building the railway from Mallow to Tralee, surnames like Naughtnane, that the timekeeper couldn't say or spell, were put down as 'Haley'. And I remember myself when I was a small child going up to Golaun to see my grandfather, an old man shoved his smig* into my face, 'You're a Kissane,' says he.

'I'm not,' I said, 'I'm a Kelly.'

'Then,' says he, 'your mother is a Kissane.'

'She's not,' I said, 'she's a Cash.'

'Oh,' he said, 'that settles it. You've the blood of the Kissane's in you. The first one of your mother's people to come here renting a bit of land, Lord Kenmare's agent asked him his name and he said, "Tadhg Ó Ciosáin".

'"What!" the agent said and put down "Cashman".

'"That's not my name," the poor man said.

'"That's the name your getting," the agent told him — "Cashman" and gave him a toe in the backside. That was his second baptism!'

For the first one like the cutting of the pock doesn't always take. People with a smattering of English, when they heard the agent shouting 'Cashman' thought he was looking for the rent already!

There was a young lad I knew baptised William and when he was born the nurse left a bandle.* Oh, that length, of a navel hanging to him. He was never called anything after only 'Two Pillie Willie'!

3
My Taggle-ee-oney

There are fashions coming out of late,
I do not know the reason,
And strange it is for to relate
They come out every season.
But a thing came out the other day,
A garment fine and homely
A pillamiloo* of a long tailed coat
And they call it the taggle-ee-oney!

Oh, I fell down and you feel down,
Is that you Paul Moloney?
You impudent brat take your leg off o' that!
That's the tail of my taggle-ee-oney.

When the sun went down the weather got cold,
You'd know by the stars 'twas freezing,
Down came the snow upon the land,
It made the scene more pleasing.
Then I went skeeting* on the ice,
The pool was deep below me.
The ice it bent and down I went
And wet my taggle-ee-oney!

Oh, I fell down and you fell down
And Yankee Doodle's pony
When he got a rub of the curry comb —
That's the tale of my taggle-ee-oney!

A maid was standing by the door,
She saw my situation.
'Young man,' she called, 'come into the fire
It will get the blood in circulation.'
So I went in and I sat down —
The flames were drying me slowly.
'Stand back!' she cried, 'you're too near the fire,
You might burn your taggle-ee-oney!'

Oh, I fell down and you fell down,
My span-new coat below me!
'Twas from Mary O'Shea I heard that song
The tale of my taggle-ee-oney!

4
The Jennet

It is often you'll hear the question asked what is the difference between a mule and a jennet. A mule is a cross between a donkey and horse and so is a jennet. In the mule's case, the mare horse is the mother and the gentleman ass is the father, and it is the other way around for the jennet, the horse is the father. Mickeen Callaghan called the offspring of that partnership a 'hybred'. Now those offspring don't breed any more, which is just as well for there are enough queer things in the world! And people will tell you that it is the lack of breeding in the lives of these hybrids which makes them very vicious. You'd want to take cover when a mule gets going with the hind legs. There is a monument put up to a mule in South Africa — they were in great demand for pulling small cannon in the Boer War. And down on this monument is written in capital letters —

THIS MULE KICKED FIFTY PRIVATES, THIRTY CORPORALS, TWENTY SERGEANTS, TEN MAJORS, FIVE CAPTAINS, TWO GENERALS AND ONE MILLS BOMB — Full stop!

In olden times, a man with a small way of living could carry an extra cow or a few more sheep if, instead of a horse, he kept a mule or a jennet; next to nothing would feed them, they were great workers and would live to be as old as Methuselah's cat.

There was this man, I won't mention his name here now, he was near enough to me, I danced at his wedding. And by the same token it was a love match too, an rud is annamh is iontach!* The girl he married, Nell Connor, because she carried no fortune in, his sister couldn't go out. Poor thing, she had to go to America after and earn it hard, and the last we heard of her was that she struck up with a Mayo lad, rotten with money, so she was lucky the creature!

But to come back to Nell Connor and the husband. They weren't too long married when they had good news, so he put a cradle making. At that time there'd be no talk of going for doctors, 'twas all home industry. Máire Bhán was the woman around here, the nurse, the bean cabhair.* It was she was everywhere, and if you didn't have whiskey inside the night she came, you'd hear about it! I remember when she was old, she used to sit up in the front of the gallery and as the people streamed into Mass she'd look down and say, 'God made ye! But it was I brought ye into the world!'

On this particular occasion complications arose and Máire Bhán got panicky, which was unusual for her, and said to the husband, 'If I was in your shoes, I'd have Nell anointed!'

In that case what'd happen is that the man'd saddle his horse and ride off to the presbytery and the parish priest or the curate'd hop in the saddle — the clergy were expert horsemen at the time — gallop back to the house and the man'd wait at the presbytery until he returned, which was a very quick operation, except in this case Nell Connor's husband had no horse: 'twas a jennet he had and he'd be there as quick walking on his knees. I suppose he was too proud to ask a neighbour for a horse, but who was visiting at the time but his nephew, a little garsún* God help him, only about seven or eight years of age. The uncle said to him, 'Here, go on now you're the youngest and the soonest to get married. Run off to the presbytery and tell the parish priest or the curate to come over as quick as they can that Nell is bad!'

The little lad was too shy to refuse and set off through strange country he had never seen before. He was given the directions. Well, the heart was being put cross-ways in the poor lad. Big dogs scattering fowl out of the yard when they saw him coming and ferocious boyos of ganders with their necks stretched out before them trying to take a bite out of his collops* at the corner of every car house — 'twas in the spring time, everyone with his own trouble!

Finally, with the life barely in him, he got to the presbytery and the housekeeper told him that the parish priest was away on a month's mind, and the curate was off on the other side of the hill on a sick call.

'But the minute he'll come,' says she, 'I'll send him back. I know where the house is; and let you be trotting off now and don't let the night overtake you on the road!'

She gave him a cut of buttered bread with sugar sprinkled on top. He ran home as hard ever as he could, he was there before the curate, and going in the yard it was a different atmosphere altogether, everyone talking and laughing. He met the cracked carpenter out against him going to Eugen's with a canteen for porter. When he went in he heard the good news: the child was born — a big beater of a baby boy, and Nell Connor sitting up in the bed drinking tea! And they were saying if the curate came now into this scene of hilarity he'd be vexed, and no wonder, bringing him on a fool's errand. So the uncle says to the garsún,* 'Look, as your legs are on the ground run back along the road and tell the curate not to come at all, that everything is all right.'

The youngster turned around, and now it was dark and going between the high hedges, he was seeing all manners of frightening objects — Sprid an Tobac* and the spirit of Balnadeega — in the bushes against the sky, and he was half crying to himself as he said, 'If my uncle had only a horse . . . dá mbeadh capall ag siúd is istigh cois tine anois a bhinn ag ól té!'*

With that he heard the horse galloping and the curate came flying round the turn. He ran out in the road and putting up his hand he shouted, 'You needn't come at all now, father, everything is all right.'

The curate, relieved, and swinging the horse on his hind legs he was about to go home, when he thought of the baptismal ceremony that'd be there in a few days time, and maybe a pound or two coming out of it. He decided that it might be polite to make some enquiry, so he said to the young lad, 'What have they?'

And the answer he got was, 'A jennet!'

5
Sprid an Tobac

An old woman used to appear at the dead of night, sitting under the eye of a bridge smoking a pipe and she was known as Sprid an Tobac.* No one'd go near the place after nightfall, they were so frightened of her until, because of some big dust-up in the world, tobacco got scarce. The smith was so bad for the want of a smoke — he claimed he was running blind — that he decided to approach Sprid an Tobac* for a couple of pulls. After a few smatháns* of the hard tack to give him courage, he went under the eye of the bridge in the middle of the night. She handed him the pipe and he took a few draws out of it, Oh the relief, and handed it back to her, saying, 'May the Lord have mercy on your soul, good woman, and on all the souls that are waiting for a glimpse of the beatific vision!'

She gave him the pipe again and he had another blast out of it and handed it back to her, praying again for her soul, even more fervently this time. She had a few draws herself before she gave it to him again and when he prayed for her a third time, she said, 'That's my purgatory over! I was made to sit here smoking — that was my punishment — until such time as someone would pray three times for my soul. I'm off to heaven,' says she, giving him a nudge and like that, she was gone up!

And it was held that it was that occurrence that gave rise to smoking at wakes! Around here the mourners took a few draws of the pipe to lighten the burden on the soul that was gone. It was at a wake I smoked my first pipeful of tobacco, and it was at the same wake I had my first taste of strong drink. I was only thirteen years of age at the time, and not being accustomed to the pipe the fumes of the tobacco smoke going down into my breadbasket were meeting the fumes of the alcohol coming up to my brain. I got very dizzy and the kitchen began to wheel about me. As I was about to faint someone said, 'Why don't you go out in the fresh air!'

'I will,' I said, 'when the door comes around again!'

6
Clever Dogs

Well, I was one night at a wake. A wake to my mind was an ideal place for storytelling, for you could suit the story to the occasion, if the man was no great loss, a little hilarity wouldn't be out of place.

A Galvin man that was dead and they were waking him at his sister's. After the visit to the room — the prayers and the condolences, 'I'm sorry for ye'r trouble. He wasn't long going in the end!' A man that had been threatening to die since he was confirmed! — I came up then and I found myself with as prime a bunch of heelers as you'd meet in a day's walk sitting below at the butt of the kitchen. Our seat was a board down on the rungs of a ladder resting on two keelers. We were out of view of the room and near the half tierce that was sitting that way on a side table with a white bucket under the tap.

As well as basins of porter there used be snuff and clay pipes going around that time. As each man or woman accepted one of these offerings he or she intoned a prayer, 'The light of heaven to us all!' or 'The Lord have mercy on his soul!' 'Amen a Thierna!'* was the usual reply to these prayers. After we had downed the second basin of porter, the conversation turned to clever dogs — you were never caught short for a topic at a wake. There was this man near me on my right. No . . . 'tis on my other side he was. A swarthy individual with a big mothal* of black hair cocking down all round under his cap. Such a fleece . . . covering his ears. Tufts of hair on his cheek bones like grass on a turtóg.* A big beard and two enormous bushy eye-brows that you could put fencing cows out of cabbage. Only for the whites of his eyes, you wouldn't know whether it was his face or his poll we were looking at. Sure, the time he was measured for false teeth, when he went back for the fitting, the dentist didn't know where to shove them! He was like a Kerry Blue he was so hairy!

When it came to his turn to talk about man's best friend, he took a slug out of the basin, settled himself and said, 'I had a very clever dog myself and his name was Bun. And I was never fonder of any dog than I was of him. I was one night above in our kitchen and I was telling about Peter Shea. There was a crowd in and my dog, Bun, was sitting there, his head on my knee, opening and closing and rolling his eyes with every twist and turn of the story, giving me as much attention as I would get from a christian, and a lot more than I would get from some of 'em, for people can allow the mind to wander. And that night I was just at the part in the story where I had Peter Shea coming back from Rome where he went for forgiveness for striking his father and everyone had his ear cocked for I'm coming to the place where he's devoured by the locusts, when, with that, one woman turns to another and in a loud voice says, "Do you hear from Hain?" I can tell you she heard from Bun! I never saw an animal so vexed! The story was ruined on him. He rounded her up and turned her out. He was used to driving sheep out on the mountain!

'That dog was as good as an extra man around the place. One morning I was driving the cattle up to the long inch. I had a little dexter cow, a breed of short-horn cattle first bred in Co. Kerry, and she was on the point of calving. But you couldn't time her. One year she'd carry three days and another year she'd carry four. I decided that morning I'd drive her up to the inch with the rest of the cattle. I did. I left Bun above in charge. I came down to the house only to find the kitchen full of people — the Toornoineach's, the wife's relations. We were talking and after a while the dog came barking into the yard. I went to the door and here was Bun outside making every motion to me to come on away with him. How could I go and the kitchen full of people, what would the wife say if I went away from the relations?

'I came in and sat down and Bun followed me in and caught me by the leg of the trousers and kept pulling me till he brought me to the door. Then when he saw that I had no notion of going with him the look of disgust that came into that dog's face. In desperation he ran down to the dairy and dipped his tail into a tub of cream and off with him the cream dripping off it. The Toornoineach's when they saw him said, "That dog is out of his mind. He's in the reels."

'We came in from the door and sat down, and for all the world it was exactly the time that Mussolini invaded Abyssinia and De Valera was over at the League of Nations trying to stop him! Well, in the middle of this discourse I heard the dog barking a second time. I ran out to the door and here was Bun coming along and a lovely little dropped calf sucking his tail and the mother of the calf walking after it.

'Such an intelligent dog. When I'd have him standing to cattle the morning of a fair I'd be lazy to go aside with myself in case he'd have 'em sold when I'd come back. But that isn't all. If I'm out working in the field and I forget my matches I have only to tell Bun go into the house and bring me out a coal of fire. Away he'd go and it is often the wife told me, "If you saw the nice handy way he'd get a hold of the sod, the red portion away from him and walk out the door with it."

'Well, I was one day ploughing the leaca* and I forgot to get matches the night before at the shop. And I said to Bun, he'd be always lying in the headland when I'd be working, "Go in," I said, "and bring me out a coal of fire."

'He went and he was a long time away, and it wasn't like him to delay when you'd send him on a message. I went up to the mouth of the poursheen* to see what was keeping him. And what was it but the wind was blowing towards the house and here was Bun coming, and he backing after his tail to keep the smoke out of his eyes!

'When Bun died my wife said to me, "you ought to be ashamed of yourself, a big fostúch* of a grown man crying after an old dog!"'

'I couldn't help it. You know the way you get attached to an animal, moreover a clever animal like a dog or a horse. Poor Bun! He was killed by a car below there at the turn of the bridge, and before he lost consciousness, with his paw, he scratched out the number of the car in the dust of the road!'

7

The Woman that went to Hell

In my father's time, when a young woman was getting married, the other women of around her own age would come to her house one night, bringing with them materials to make a patchwork quilt, and this quilt when it was made was a present for the young wife to bring to her new home.

They had a quilting frame that time on which to stretch the base and cover of the new quilt. Then one clever lady with an eye for design would take a splinter from the fire, let the burnt end cool, and with this draw out the shapes on the cover. Each woman was given a section to work at, and she'd take out the odds and ends of coloured materials cutting them in various shapes according to fancy while the supervising lady moved the pieces around to get a nice balance of colour and so on.

As the women sewed up and down, they'd put a lot of packing between the base and the cover, bits and scraps of worn garments, a piece of an old woollen drawers, anything there was heat in. And when they were finished, some of those quilts were so heavy you'd nearly want to get artificial respiration after coming out from under them.

There would be great jollity among the women as they worked and talked of comical and strange happenings, and talk of courting and talk of love, for it was shrove time and matrimony was in the air. You'd hear talk of the man that went to hell for the flail. The journey was made possible by three things which he got from a knowledge-able woman. One was a piece of leather no longer than a haime's strap, which when he'd squeeze on it, would lift him up and take him in whatever direction it was pointed, and so as to be able to withstand the high temperature below, the second thing she gave him was ointment in a round, tin, car-grease box. This ointment he was to rub into himself all over, but there was one spot between the shoulder blades which he couldn't reach, so he threw a dollop of it at the wall and rubbed his back to it. The third thing she gave him was a flute which when he'd play it the devils couldn't stop dancing. The only tune he knew was, 'If I had a Wife that I didn't like'. He struck it up as soon ever as he got inside the gate below, and all the devils fell in to knocking sparks out of the flag stones of hell. He took the flail, a miraculous weapon that could do the work of ten men. He brought it home where in time he made a fortune hiring himself out to big farmers threshing oats in the fall of the year.

The night before Dydeo Moriarty got married his wife-to-be came to the house. She wanted him to promise that he'd support her mother as well as herself. Dydeo Moriarty was not a very generous individual but this young woman was the only woman he wanted as a wife, and, even though it went against the grain in him to do it, he made the promise. He lived to regret his promise. Very soon he got sick of the wife's mother. His house wasn't his own; from the time she put her leg inside the door she was ordering and bossing him, and at the table she had as big a stroke as a man that'd be mowing! So he said to the wife that the mother would have to go.

'All right,' the wife said, 'I knew it would come to this. But I can't turn her out now the weather is so cold. I'll make some warm clothes for her and then she can go.'

They agreed to that. At that time you wouldn't walk into the shop and order a rig-out. No. The wife had a few sheep shorn and the wool washed and carded and spun on the old spinning-wheel near the fire, and warped on the warping-frame and the thread taken to the weaver to be woven into cloth. Then the material was brought home and cut and sewn so that an enormous length of time had gone by before the mother was finally togged out.

'Is she going now?' says Dydeo.

'She's going now,' the wife said, 'and I'm going with her!'

'Don't you go at all,' says Dydeo. ''Tis how I couldn't support the two of ye!'

'How could you support a family so?' says the wife, pulling the shawl out over her head, and herself and her mother went off down the road.

'You are well rid of him,' the mother said to the daughter as they went along. 'A padhsán.* I never liked the táthaire.'*

They kept going, the two of them, a bite here and a sup there, until after about a week, they struck into a big farmer's house. They stayed the night there and the following morning it was lashing out of the heavens — you wouldn't put out a dog.

'Can't you stay where you are!' the farmer said to the young woman. 'Yourself and your mother. I am short of servants anyway to work in the kitchen.'

So they remained on. The farmer had another big house at the other side of the farm, and from what was known, anyone that spent the night there was found dead in the morning. Because of some evil occurrence there was a curse on the place. The farmer didn't let on about this but he asked the young woman would she spend a night in the house and she, thinking that there must be something at the back of it, said she would if he gave her enough money and crossed her palm with silver. That was all right, the bargain was made and she went alone to the house. She put down a fine fire and sat up beside it and good enough, about two o'clock in the morning there was a knock at the door. She wanted to know who was outside.

'You don't know me at all,' the voice said. 'Open the door!'

She opened the door and there was a young man there and he drove a cow into the kitchen before him, and taking a vessel he told her to milk the cow and drink the first of the milk and to go out then and throw the rest of it against the wind. She milked the cow, drank the first of it and walked out and threw the rest of it against the wind. He didn't say another word, only drove the cow out of the kitchen and was gone, and there was no more commotion for the rest of the night. When she went back to the farmer in the morning, she could see by the stand in his eyes that he was very anxious to know what transpired. And there and then she made up her mind that she'd keep what she saw to herself for a while anyway.

'Are you all right?' he said.

'I am,' says she.

'Did you see anything?'

'No,' says she. 'I didn't see anything — I didn't see anything unusual.'

'Would you go there again tonight?' he said.

'I will,' says she, 'If you double the money.'

The money was doubled and she spent the second night there and the same thing happened. When she said to the farmer in the morning that she didn't see anything he seemed to be disappointed. He asked her would she go the third night. She said she would if the amount of money was doubled again. She got all the money into her hand, and at dusk that evening when the crows were noising overhead, she set out for the strange house. She put a fine fire down. She was so used to the place now that she went to bed and sure enough, on the stroke of two, the knock came to the door. She didn't ask at all who was there this time, she let him in, milked the cow, drank the first of the milk and threw the rest of it against the wind. He drove the cow out and as he was turning on his heel to go, she said, 'What hurry are you in? There's a fine fire here!'

He put his hand to the door and closing it out he came in and sat down. In the morning, when the young woman came to the farmer, she asked him if she could stay at the house now altogether and bring her mother too. This was agreed and herself and her mother lived there except that the young woman came each day and worked in the kitchen for the farmer. This went on, as the old storytellers used to say for three spaces of time, trí ráithe,* until one morning the young woman did not come to work for the farmer.

'As sure as anything 'tis dead she is,' the farmer said to his wife, so the two set out for the strange house only to find the young woman, propped up in the bed and a big poltóg* of a young child dancing on her lap and there at the head of the bed was the cowboy! The farmer and his wife went white with terror. They knew him well, and why wouldn't they for he was their dead son that had been brought back from the grave by some power, the working of which we are better off not to know.

There was a belief in the old religion that the dead came back for a favourite animal and I was given the man's name that came back for his horse. The two men that saw him were standing inside by the manger late at night when the dead man's spirit came in the door — they knew him as well as I know you — and walking up the spirit laid his hand on the horse's mane and ran it down along his spine. The horse rolled over and died and two white objects sailed out the door. That incident was told to me by Timmy Callaghan, a man that's dead himself now, and I would not belie him.

But to get back to the farmer. When he and his wife got over the shock of seeing their dead son they said to him, 'Where were you since?' and he said he was in hell.

'Now that you are restored to life,' the farmer said, 'and able to do things!' looking at the child, 'you'll remain with us!'

'I can't, I've seven years more to do in hell,' the son told them. 'If I don't go they'll come for me!'

'Don't go from us!' they said to him.

'Look,' the father said, 'I'm an old man now my race is run. I'll go for the seven years in your place!'

It was arranged as things could be arranged that time and that old man went straight down to hell, but it wasn't long until he was back screeching and roaring and they had to throw buckets of water on him to quench him. The mother said she'd go. 'The men have no bearing of the heat anyway!' she said. She stuck it for a few days. Then the young woman said, 'It's up to me. I'll go!'

God help us! That young girl wanted most of all to be with her small child, but she went down into the black pit of hell. A dark valley with high burning buildings, red windows and devils looking out of every window. For seven years she suffered in the fires of hell and when the seven years were up the authorities came to her and said, 'If you remain on here for three more years any amount of souls will be set free the day you are going!'

Her inclination was to go home and see her child but then she asked herself the question — was there any other woman anywhere in a position to do the same amount of good that she could do? And knowing what the suffering in hell was like she decided, for the sake of the souls that would be freed, to remain on. Every minute was an hour, every hour was a day, every day was a week and every week was a year. But the time came and she was set free and so many souls were let out of hell that you could hardly draw a leg the traffic was so thick coming up the stairs. On the second landing who should she meet coming down against her but her first husband Dydeo Moriarty and it came to the tip of her tongue to shout down to the devils, 'Shove him into the blackest hole below!'

But she curbed her tongue. She came back to this world and went straight away to the farmer's house. When she went in the door the farmer and his wife were dressing up as if for a journey. They didn't know her at all.

'Where are ye going?' she said.

'Well, 'tis this way,' says the farmer, 'I've another house at the other end of the farm and my son is getting married there tonight.'

Oh Dia linn!* This was something she didn't expect and she didn't know what to do!

'Can I go over with ye?' she said.

They didn't raise any objection, and when they got over to the other house, the crowds were collecting for the wedding . . . the priest's horse coming into the yard. The minute she went inside the kitchen door, she looked around to see would she see her child that was only a few day's old when she went away. There was a young lad of about ten years of age playing with a castle top on the flag of the hearth, and she was wondering could this be her son. When she sat down, the little boy came over to her and they were talking and this was unusual for at that time children were uncommonly shy. She looked up to see the father of the child watching her. He had changed like she had, ten years is a long time, so that for a while they were doubtful of each other. When he realised who she was, he ran over and put his two hands around her. The father and mother of the bride-to-be, when they saw that, had pusses on them from here down to the door and wanted an explanation.

'There'll be no marriage now,' he said, 'because the woman I thought I'd never see again, the woman that restored me to life and the mother of my child, has come back to me! But as the food is prepared, it would be a pity to waste it! So let what began as a wedding party, end up as a hauling home!'

8
Tóg Bog É!*

When I was a young lad there was a man living here. The devil, I never heard any other name for him only Tóg Bog É.* Not that he was lazy or disinclined to work, for he was not, only that he kept his private affairs very much to himself, and if you were to press him for information about domestic occurrences, he'd say, 'Ah, Tóg bog é anois!'* To give you an example of the man. He was coming from the fair one day after selling a cow and he met a neighbour on the road and the neighbour said to him, 'What class of a fair was it?'

'Only a middling fair, then.'

'I see you sold the cow.'

'I did.'

'What did you get for her?'

'O . . . h! Tóg bog é anois!'*

'Well, did you get what you expected?'

'No then,' he said, 'or I didn't expect I would.'

Wouldn't he make a star witness at a murder trial! He didn't get married until late in life. He was too shy when he was young and nearly too old when he got the courage. And he'd be left there altogether, and die wondering as many did in those days, only that his relations came together and made it up between himself and Tidy Womaneen. She was called that because when she was young she was a lovely pudgy, small, fat little lump of a baby, and her grandmother used to be bouncing her up and down on her knee and singing to her:

*Tidy womaneen, tidy womaneen, tidy womaneen sásta,**
Milked the cow in the tail of her gown

and left it there until morning.
Throw her up and up and up,
Throw her up in the sky,
Throw her up and up and up,
And she'll come down bye 'n' bye.
She didn't dance and dance,
She didn't dance all day . . .

and I don't know any more of it! And I never laughed so many, as the fellow said, and you would laugh if all belonging to you were laid out in front of you, the night that Tóg Bog É went over to look at Tidy Womaneen. He had a couple of the neighbours with him to give him courage. There was Jur Gorman and a few more and they were walking up and down outside her house — 'twas dark. Tóg Bog É was talking very loud — whistling passing the graveyard! — referring to the blight on the potatoes and how many times the crop should be sprayed. And that was the time the knapsack sprayer came in, and the improvement it was on the bunch of heather, spattering it on the stalks like holy water: and they were arguing about how many pounds of blue stone you should put to so many pounds of washing soda to get the right spraying stuff, and no two of them on the same word. And Jur Gorman in the middle of all this said to Tóg Bog É, 'Did you see the woman yet?' Of course this'd be the last consideration!

'No then,' says Tóg Bog É, 'I didn't.'

'Maybe,' says Jur, 'she'd be in this bunch coming down.'

There was a bunch of girls the breadth of the road coming down against them.

'We'll stop 'em, ' he said. And they did.

'There she is,' says he, 'the one in the middle.'

Tóg Bog É only cracked a match like that, and held it up in front of her face, and then turning to Jur Gorman, he said, 'Why then you can overdo the blue stone!'

Wouldn't you think that that was the wrong approach to matrimony. 'Twas not, for there's no understanding women. Whatever she saw in his eye in the light of the match, she fell head over heels in love with him! And he responded — took to courtship like an ass to clover. They got married and he brought her home where everything in the garden was velvet. Well, not everything. There were two flies in the ointment. Tóg Bog É's mother and Tóg Bog É's eldest sister Eily that never settled down — she was always there in the house. And the two of them were tall and thin, long, lanky and lonesome as the man said. For all the world the same as if you put a petticoat on the tongs!

And do you know, it galled them to have a strange woman inside on their floor and it killed them down dead to see her hand inside in their tea canister. They were watching every single thing that she did and they were criticising everything she did. She was of a very quiet disposition, poor Tidy Womaneen — a nice, nacoss,* friendly, accommodating, small little lump of humanity — and she didn't say anything, another woman'd be dug out of the two of them. Or she didn't even say a word about it to Tóg Bog É. How did she know but that he might take sides with them — as if it didn't often happen.

Things went from bad to worse and Tidy Womaneen couldn't stick life any longer with these two frowning viragos, so Tóg Bog É woke up one morning to find himself alone in the hammock — the bird had flown! And then the thing was, because of the secretive nature of the man, to keep the disgrace from the neighbours. And if you went into that house the following day or the day after, Tóg Bog É would be inside wetting tea and shouting up in the room, 'Would you like a bit of toast with it?'

You'd know by the way she was above!

But the neighbours know what's going on — you couldn't take out the pot unknown to them. This was brought home to Tóg Bog É in a very comical fashion. He was at the fair. He was buying a springer and he was a very tough man to make a bargain too — maybe ye don't know what I'm talking about? A springer is not a thing for putting off a rocket. 'Tis a thing you'd milk, a cow about to calf.

'Twas about eleven o'clock in the morning and he hadn't the little cow bought; then he saw Jur of the Hill and Jur of the Hill had a small black cow that'd suit Tóg Bog É's place down to the ground. She'd be able to fend for herself among the rocks. He asked Jur how much was he looking for for the cow.

'Sixteen pounds,' he said. Tóg Bog É offered him ten, and Jereen, oh an awful man with the tongue, said, 'Suffering duck, I wouldn't wake her out of her sleep for that!'

Tóg Bog É went up a pound, two pounds and three pounds, but Jur of the Hill would not come down! Finally, after an awful bout of words in which they threw every asacán* at one another, Tóg Bog É offered him thirteen pounds ten. But Jur wouldn't take it. And Tóg Bog É, his face blackening with bad temper, for he fancied the cow, said, 'You can take her home so!'

'I will,' says Jur of the Hill, 'and what's more, she'll stay with me too!'

I can tell you that knocked a hop out of Tóg Bog É and he said to himself, 'If it is known on the hill, it is known in the hollow. I won't deny it anymore!'

That evening over a few drinks, he asked the advice of a long-headed man about getting back Tidy Womaneen for he was miserable without her, and what he was told was to drive the mother and the sister, Eily, down in the room, wall up the door and break out another door in the gable for them. This he did and when Tidy Womaneen heard that she was going to be queen of her own section of the palace, she came back to him. And there was a no more devoted pair! If you saw them back there in town linking arms! So much so that strangers were asking who they were, and they were told. Tóg and Mrs Bog É!

9
The Golaun's

My great grandfather, Seana* Neid, in his young days knew
no English only what he'd use for a fair or market day. He
was up before the court one time, and when he came
home, the neighbours wanted to know how he got on.

'I took the stand,' he said, 'and cased my state!'

Seana Neid seemed to like the court for often when he
had a few drinks in, he used abuse the peelers and he used
to be hauled up for using language likely to lead to a
breach of the peace. So his English must be improving!

He was called one time as a witness in a will case.
Seemingly the relations that didn't benefit from the will
wanted to make out that the dead man was of unsound
mind when he made it. Seana Neid was called by the ben-
eficiaries and the attorney for the non-beneficiaries turning
to my great grandfather, when he took the stand, said, 'Is
it not a fact that the deceased was given to soliloquising?'

Seana Neid said nothing. Smiled at the judge. Although
he remarked to someone in private after that it was well
known the man died sudden!

'I'm afraid,' the judge said to the attorney, 'you'll have
to simplify your question for the witness.'

And the attorney, who, no doubt became a judge himself after, put it another way.

'Is it not a fact,' he said to Seana Neid, 'that the dead
man talked to himself when alone?'

'I don't know,' Seana Neid said. 'I was never with him
when he was alone!'

The Golaun's, that's where he came from, were very lazy
to use Irish in town for the crowd inside, the townies'd be

only making fun of them. Although it was said that in the lanes, up Bóthairín Caol and over Bóthairín Dannehy the very poor people knew Irish. But you can be sure the man with the polished boot was making fun of those too.

'Give over your cadrawling* in Irish,' a shopkeeper said to Seana Neid one day. 'We all talks the best of the king's English here.'

'Why then, if the king walked in the door now,' says Seana Neid, 'I don't think he'd understand what you are saying!'

It was amazing the rapidity with which the people picked up English that time. They had to. To get away to America. Some of them learned their English over, and they didn't pine away for want of someone to talk to in their own lingo while they were learning it, for there was as much Irish spoken in New York then as there was in the province of Munster. But they never let on to the foreigner that their people at home spoke Irish. And my uncle's father-in-law's father was telling me that there was this girl and she married an English man with a top notch position and in time they had a little bonóicín* — a baby girl. God help us, what the grandparents at home wouldn't give to see the child so they decided to take a trip home. But the daughter wrote to the mother beforehand, saying, 'Tell Dada and the lads not to have any Irish in the house during the visit.'

So, duirt sí le Dada and the lads gan aon Ghaolainn a labhairt ós chomhair an tSasanaigh. Bhí go maith agus bhí go holc leis.* They arrived and everything was fine and civilised — no Irish until the old woman, who had been to the spout for water, got a glimpse of the baby. All the good resolutions not to talk Irish went by the board and hugging the child she said: 'O mo chircín! Mo chircín circ! A stór mo chroí istigh. Dia do bheannacha a laogh, a leanbhín gleoite!'*

Then seeing the look of consternation on her daughter's face, she knew the fat was in the fire and drawing English to herself in a hurry the old lady proclaimed, 'You're nate, Nate out. God blast you!'

Of course the big argument to get people to give up talking Irish that time was, 'What good is it to you when you'll g'out?' I don't know. There were these two brothers and they were walking from Birmingham down to London and when they got to Dunstable that's there near Luton, they spent the last few bob they had on a bite of dinner. They were broke then, if you could describe people as broke who had nothing starting. They fooled around the town until they came to a place where there was a side-show, and a big prize being offered to the person that could eat the most chickens at the one sitting.

Now one of the brothers was so huge, a fine ball of a man, that he could hardly come in the door and the other fellow was so small he could nearly come in through the keyhole. Two chickens was the most devoured by any man entering for the prize so far. They put in for the competition, the big fellow to eat the chickens and the small fellow to act as his second and to see that the big man'd get fair play.

They took their place on the platform and the first chicken was handed up to the big man. He began to wire into it, and when he was half-way through he turned and said to the brother in Irish, 'Nac é an trua go deo é go raibh an dinnéar againn!'* bemoaning the fact that they had the dinner!

'What did he say?' says the judge to the small fellow.

'As nice a chicken as he ever tasted, sir!'

He finished that chicken and the second one was handed up to him. He began with the legs, then the wings and he was getting encouragement now from the crowd, and do you know that encouragement is as good a sauce as anything. He finished the second chicken. A big cheer from the crowd as the third chicken was handed up. If he

finished this one he'd be the winner. But the small lad
knew by the look on the big man's face, and he knew from
the way he was chewing, and the lazy way he was swal-
lowing that the edge had gone off his appetite. And with a
good three-quarters of the chicken to go the big man
turned to his brother and said, 'Is baolach ná deanfad an
gnó!'*

'What did he say?' says the judge.

'That he could do for three more!' says the small fellow.

'Ah give him the money,' says the judge. 'That fellow'd
ate us out of house and home!'

10
Dean Swift and his Serving Man

When Dean Swift was going round Ireland on horseback, from what we hear the food he got in the lodging-houses did not agree with him! No knowing the amount of bread soda the poor man consumed to alleviate the effects of bad cooking. So the Dean decided to bring his serving man with him the next time he was going around Ireland comforting the people. He was more in need of comforting himself! It so happened that they were passing through Cork and they put up in a lodging house in Washington Street. Dean Swift had always the name of having a great eye for the women, agus do bhí cara mná tí aige an oiche seo i Sráid Bhaisinton,* and this lady, when they were parting company in the small hours, gave him the present of a fat goose. What you might call a happy woman!

The Dean gave the goose to the serving man next morning to prepare her for the dinner. The serving man plucked the goose and cleaned out the goose and stuffed the goose and clapped her down in the big bastible oven over the fire — they used to have the use of the kitchen in any house they'd be staying in.

This way up in the parlour the Dean was, reading and writing and taking it easy after the night. Now, the serving man was so taken up with the goose, turning her in the bastible and spooning the gravy over her, and putting strips of bacon, like saddle pieces on her back to add to the flavour, that the goose was nearly done before he thought of putting down the spuds. So he put the bastible to the side, and he washed the spuds and put them down. It took the potatoes an awful long time to do, and the serving man's belly was nearly back to his spine with the hunger as he gave every second glance at the goose, and the lovely smell, and the little bubbles winking in the gravy all round her. In the end, his patience gave out and taking hold of the goose, he broke off one of the legs and made a mouth organ of it. And then looking at the goose, and the cut of her with only one leg, he got guilty but what was the good, the harm was done now.

Finally when the spuds boiled, he strained them and brought the pot down in the parlour and turned them all out on a bageen cloth, and himself or Dean Swift couldn't see one another across the table with the steam rising out of them! He came then and he knocked the goose on the flat of her back on a big plate and landed her that way o'er right the Dean out, and the two of them sat in to the table.

The Dean, noticing that the goose had only one leg said, 'Explain this to me!'

'Ah,' says the serving man, 'that's the kind of geese they have here in Cork. They never have but the one leg under 'em!'

The Dean, a knowledgeable man, didn't say anymore. The two of them fell in and finished every morsel of what was on the table before them. Well, the appetites men had at that time!

The following morning they were on their way back to Dublin. A frosty morning it was too, you could hear the echoing of the horses' hoofs going up Glanmire. There was a pond covered with ice at the side of the road with a squad of geese on it. And as is their habit in the cold, the geese were standing on one leg, the other one tucked up inside the wing warming. The horsemen pulled up.

'There you are now,' says the serving man, 'do you see the comrades of the goose on the plate last night. Only one-legged geese in Cork!'

The Dean shoved over near them and striking his two hands together, he said, 'Coosh!'

With that every goose there put her second leg under her.

'Now!' says the Dean with great glee, 'are they all one-legged?'

'Ah but,' says the serving man, 'you didn't say "coosh" to the goose on the plate!'

11
I am a Young Fellow

I am a young fellow that's run out of land and means,
*Is Caileacha an bhaile ní thabharach dom bean ná spré,**
I placed my affections on one that had gold and store,
*Is do gheallas don ainir go leanfainn í féin go deo.**

We made up our minds with each other for to elope,
*Is do dhíreas mo chapall i gcoinnibh mo mhíle stór.**
I met my true lover just at the appointed place,
*Is do shroiceamair Caiseal ar maidin le h-eirí an lae.**

When we reached into Cashel she called for a quart of ale,
*Is coirce don chapall, is uisge, is a dhóthain féir.**
She opened her purse and she pulled out a note to change,
*Is bhí cead agus dathad do ghiní breá buí ag an mbéib.**

In Waterford city we stripped and our clothes we changed,
*Is do dhíolas mo chapall le sagart ó pharóiste an tsléibh.**
The ship it was ready, the weather it was fine and clear,
*Is d'fhágmair an talamh gan eagla ná gá ná baol.**

When we reached into London the polis were on the quay.
*Bhí na barántaisí scríte san 'Telegraph News' ó inné!**
We both were arrested and taken at once to gaol,
*Agus tugadh ar ais sin go Cluain Mealla chun ár gcúis do thrial.**

The day of my trial her mother she swore severe.
*Go n-ólfainn mo thuileamh ag imeacht le h-aer an t-saoil.**
That her daughter was simple and I was a scheming rake,
*Is gur bhuaileas an bob uirthe i gan fhios don saol go léir.**

The jury assembled and the judge to expound the law,
Is d'fhiafruidear don ainir cad a bhí aici fein le rá *
She said that I was a most humble, genteel young swain,
Is na bpósadh sí a mhalairt go sínfí í sios faoin gcré. *

We both were acquitted. I went my true lover to embrace,
Is chuamar chun sagairt chun ceangail le grá mo chléibh. *
The knot it was tied, it was simple, I took my change,
Agus mairimear sásta gan eagla ná gá ná baol! *

That is one of the many songs that came out of the change
over from Irish to English. Half and half songs I call them.
Jack Leahy, who had a hedge school out the Muckross
road, made up some including *One Day for Recreation,*

> *If I had you in a nate grove*
> *Idir Clydagh agus Muckross,* *
> *Your sparkling eyes do taze me,*
> *Trí lár mo chroí tá taithneamh duit!* *

I met a man from Clydagh once and he told me he was the
youngest of a family of twenty. I remember him telling me
that when his eldest brother started to talk it was all Irish
that was in the house, and when he began to talk himself
English was the everyday speech. That man didn't know a
single word of Irish. He was scuffling mangolds in the
field as I came down the road and I shouted into him,
'Dia's Muire dhuit!'*
'Straight on,' he said, 'You can't miss it!'
And how can you account for the fact that his family
slid from Irish to English in the time between the births of
the first and twentieth child? The Clydagh man explained
it to me.
'The desire,' he said, 'to get on in the world outside is
strong in people of no property, and after the establishment
of the National Schools many parents that were able to

string a few words of English together didn't speak any more Irish to their children. They'd as soon give them the itch as give them Irish. Although when the neighbours came visiting they spoke Irish among themselves around the fire, but they'd hunt the children out of ear shot in case they'd pick it up. "Rise! Get up," the parents'd say. "G'out! Go abroad. There's no rain on it!"

'The only time they'd ever turn to Irish in front of the children was when they had some local gossip or scandal to hide. And people like those, caught in a gap between two languages, could sound awful funny to the Irish speakers they were trying to run away from, as well as the English speakers they were trying to catch up to.'

I asked the Clydagh man if he had ever heard of Jack and Jer Balbh.* He had of course, everyone heard of the Balbhs. Brothers they were and Jack had some schooling. He claimed to have gone as far as, 'Can a snail walk?' in the second book. Naturally a man of his learning spoke only English. At supper-time in the winter he was often heard to say to the brother, 'Scarce the milk, Jer, the cow is going thirsty!'

Jack and Jer had only a small way of living, one cow, but they weren't altogether depending on her as they had an income from the services of a gentleman goat. And to make these services more widely known and therefore more lucrative they decided to make out a notice and hang it on the chapel gate. This they did, and when the parish priest read the notice he nearly lost his cork leg, for what they had written down was —

> Us have puck. Us charge sixpence for the pucking,
> But if the goat comes second rutting,
> Us will puck that goat for nothing!

12

Eoghan Rua Ó Súilleabháin Finds an English-speaking Son-in-law for a Wealthy Farmer

Eoghan Rua Ó Súilleabháin, the poet, was out walking one day and he called into a rich farmer's house. An only daughter was all the farmer had and he was on the look out for a cliamhain isteach* for her. But the farmer would not be satisfied with any son-in-law, only a young man that could talk English.

That was a stiff enough proposition at the time — two hundred years ago. But even then, English was thought to be a leg up for the man that wanted to rise and be well thought of in the world. The farmer told Eoghan, and he told the right man, that he was having trouble getting an English-speaker for the daughter, and did Eoghan know of anyone.

Eoghan said he did — go raibh aithne aige ar gharsún mín macánta,* but the pity of it was he could not come into such a fine house, having no fortune.

'Don't mind about the fortune,' says the farmer, 'if he can talk English won't we all be learning from him.'

'The way it is,' says Eoghan, 'the English isn't good by him, but if you look at it another way, the English isn't bad by him.'

'Can't you bring him here to the house,' says the farmer, 'and we'll see!'

Eoghan went off and he never drew rein until he met a fine strapping young man that had neither land nor means nor English. Eoghan brought him along to his own house, put a good suit of clothes on him and gave a few days tutoring him up on how to give a perfect answer in English to a question Eoghan was going to ask him.

When the young man had mastered the piece of English, the two, Eoghan and the young man, set out for the farmer's house. There was a big crowd there that night. All talking away in Irish. The young lad, when he went in, made off with the farmer's daughter, a nice little mallet of a one, and in no time the two of them were whispering and conoodling in the corner.

Out in the night, as was pre-arranged, Eoghan gave the young man the nod and he went out in the yard. When he was gone, Eoghan said to the farmer in Irish, 'I suppose you're anxious to hear this young man talking in English?'

'Isn't that what we are here for,' says the farmer.

'He is gone out there now,' says Eoghan. 'I'll put some talk on him when he comes in.'

When the young man had done whatever it was he went out to do, he turned back and when he was noising at the door Eoghan says to him, 'Well, friend and what are the climatic conditions abroad?'

On hearing this, the young man straightened himself, and clapping one eye on the farmer's daughter he said, 'From my astronomical observations, from my reckoning and my calculations, from the widespread fermentation of the atmosphere, the constant rolling of the firmament and the dismal aspect of the stars, I prognosticate a heavy discharge from the clouds!'

'Good,' says Eoghan. 'I find your peregrinations most pertinent to behold!'

Well, the farmer was there and his mouth opened back to his two ears, you could put a turnip into it. Anything foreign impresses the Irish!

'Ó,' ar seisean, 'nach iontach go deo an t-urlabhra an Béarla. D'fhanfainn ag eisteacht leis an gcainnt sin go lá an Luain!' *

The young man's English was so good no one had the courage to engage him in conversation. The farmer thought he was a professor out of Trinity Hall. There was no trouble in making the match but they weren't too long married when the farmer found out that that was all the English he had. The farmer had a pain in his head from 'the widespread fermentation of the atmosphere'.

Came the big fair at Knocknagree and the farmer and the daughter were there standing to a cow, when who should come down the street but the poet, Eoghan Rua, singing one of his new compositions. The farmer ran out in front of him and caught him by the two lapels of the coat and gave him a good shaking. 'You blackguard of the world,' says he, 'and the way you codded me!'

'Take it easy now,' says Eoghan, 'don't be running away with yourself! What's wrong?'

'Didn't you tell me,' says the farmer, 'that that bodach* of a son-in-law knew English!'

'I told you no such thing,' says Eoghan. 'Recollect yourself! Didn't I say to you that the English wasn't good by him?'

'You did,' says the farmer.

'And didn't I say to you the English wasn't bad by him?' says Eoghan.

'You did,' says the farmer.

'And didn't I say to you so that he had no English *good* nor *bad*!'

Turning to the daughter, Eoghan said to her: 'Do you find any fault with him?'

'No,' says she. 'But of course 'tisn't for English I want him!'

13

The Man that never Slept

When my Auntie Nora came home from America . . . I don't know now was that the first or the second trip. Anyway, her husband was with her and they stayed here. We did up the room below, broadened the window and put in a boarded floor, for the stone flags are cold to put your bare feet on when you get out of the bed in the morning. We put down a blazing fire for it is common knowledge that the yanks do complain about the damp.

Nora's husband was mad to be off sight-seeing every day in the pony and trap. He was American born and as the country was new to him, he couldn't see enough of it. We went one day to the seaside and for the bite to eat we dined in a house on the knob of a hill. There was an old man by the fire and I knew by the glint in his eye that he had any amount of talk if he could be tapped.

There was a ruin of what looked like a mansion between us and the strand, you could see it through the open door. When Nora and the husband went out to see the sights, I said that there must be some story attached to the mansion. The old man said there was. He told me the name of the man who built it.

'An only son is all he had and when the house was finished the father went to great trouble to get a nice young woman for the son. She was from the country up, all belonging to her very respectable it seems. She came to live in that house below, and while she was there she never wet her fingers, or she had no need to, for she had plenty of servants.

'No day passed that she didn't go swimming alone in the sunny cove beside the house. You can't see it from here now. It is well cut off from view. The only place you'd see it right, is if you were in a boat out on the waves. Every day, as I said, she went in swimming by herself. According to the servants and those who had recourse to the house, the young couple were happy out. Plenty of money anyway, no complaints in that line. The only thing was, the years were going by on wings and they had no family. They must be about ten years married when one evening she came in from the sea, and when she stood in the door the servants knew that something had happened to her, for as the storyteller put it: Bhí aiteas agus scannra uirthi — she was strange and frightened. She was put to bed and she got all the attention they could give her and nine months after a child was born to her. The old women that were there that night said he was a remarkable child, very beautiful. A boy it was and the parents, and indeed the grandparents, were delighted with him. Every day and every night that went by, the child improved until he was as fine a young man as ever walked down that road outside.

'But there was one thing and it was a strange thing, he never slept. He'd go to bed the same as you or me but since the day he was born, he never closed an eye.

'Now it happened one fine summer's evening, his father and grandparents were dead by this time, a travelling scholar came to the house looking for lodgings.

'"Come in, poor scholar," the young man said.

The scholar did and he put his books down. The supper was going and he was invited to sit into the table. "Cabáiste Scotch"* they had: they'd put down a head of white cabbage and when it was done, they had an affair to squeeze the water out of it. Then they'd cut it up small, mix in chopped onions, add some cream you had left go sour, pepper and salt and put it outside on the wall to cool — it was no damn good unless it was cold. Then peel a big floury spud and with a little pat of butter on it, plank it down in the middle and with a mug of buttermilk you did have a supper!

'When everyone had enough, the young man of the house told the servants to go away to bed now and himself and the scholar remained up, well into the night, putting the world to and fro.

'"You'd be asleep long ago only for me," says the scholar, making a move to rise.

'"You wouldn't say that if you knew me," the young man said. "I don't know what it is like to sleep, for I never slept in my life."

'"There's something very mysterious about that," says the scholar. "I never heard anything like it!"

'"You are a man of great knowledge," the young man said to him, "so why don't you open your books and see if there's any class of people on this earth who never slept."

'The scholar drew his books to him and many is the hour he spent over them and finally he said to the young man, "In all I've read, I can find only a bare reference to a people of that nature, but they no longer live on the surface of the earth for their land was swallowed by the sea!"

'"I'll pay you well for your trouble," the young man said, "go to bed now, 'tis late!"

'The bed for the poor was near the fire, so the scholar lay down and closed his eyes and the young man watched him until his breathing was even and he was sound asleep. He went up then to where his mother slept.

'"What's troubling you, son?" she said, waking up when he came into the room.

'"There's something I want to ask you!" he said, talking very quiet so that he wouldn't wake anyone.

'"I'll answer it if I can," she said.

'"How long were you and my father married before I was born?"

'"I thought I often told you, son. It was ten years," she said.

'"And you had nothing to do with any other man only my father? Tell me the truth!" he said when she wasn't answering him.

'"I was never with another man," she said. "But I have something to tell you, which I could never bring myself to tell before. I was one day swimming in that cove below, I was so accustomed to the sea at the time, that I could swim for a good spell under the wave as well as on it. I knew every little cave along by Faill na nGabhar*, and often I dived down to bring a fancy shell up from the sea bed. The day I'm telling you about, as I swam I thought there was someone by my side. I looked and there was no one there; the water was clear all round but I had the feeling that there was someone near me. Imagine the fear that came over me when on looking down to where the sun threw my shadow on the bed of the sea, I saw a second shadow that moved with mine which ever way I turned. The two shadows came together as I swam in to the strand, where I dropped down at the brink of the tide so tired that I fell asleep. When I came up to the house after, everyone was worried about me I was out so long. I was put to bed, three spaces of time passed and you were born."

'He left the room and in the morning when they all had broken their fast together, he went to where he kept his money, and he paid the scholar for the information. The land, he divided up among his servants, and left the mansion and plenty to do his mother while she'd live. He parted with her then, and it broke her heart to see him take his coat and make for the door.

'"I'm sorry to go," he said, "but I have to go to my own people."

'A big crowd followed him down to the strand, where he went into the sea and swam out. And the people there saw a man rise up out of the waves and embrace the young man and together they swam left by the black rock until they were out of sight.'

And that is the story as I heard it, without adding to it or taking from it, the day I went to the seaside in the pony and trap with my Auntie Nora and her husband when they were home on their second trip from Springfield, Mass.

After a night's talk in this house long ago when the visitors'd rise to go, my father'd see them to the door. If the night was bright they'd stand a while looking up the rising countryside wondering what sort of weather to-morrow would bring. Every field up there had a name at the time, and some little story of its own to make it different from any other field. So had every prominent rock and every stream. Up there you'll find Loch an Dá Bhó Dheag — the Twelve Cow Lake, which got its name from an Ghlas Ghaibhneach, a very beautiful and mysterious cow that gave a never ending supply of milk for the poor. She was highly productive! The old people used to say that the field in which she grazed and slept and manured remained fertile forever more.

But some prime boyo, we are told, sold her milk to line his own pocket! This was sacrilege as far as the cow was concerned. So she called together her eleven daughters ranging in ages from eleven years to a yearling heifer and cocking their tails they put the hill up out of them, and jumped into the lake leaving a greedy world behind them.

Show Loch an Dá Bhó Dheag to any young lad living here now and ask him the name of it and he'll tell you that's 'the lake'. Show him Páirc a'tSasanaigh,* and he'll tell you that's 'the field'. Cnoc an Áir* is 'the hill' and the glaise* that runs down to the Abhann Uí Chraidha* is 'the stream' that flows into 'the river'. Like my ancestor, Tadhg Ó Ciosáin, the changing world has left them without a name and without a story.

If you walk up there in the day time you'll find remnants of houses under the briars and ferns. You can trace the room and kitchen, the yard, the cróitín* where they kept the cow, and the ridges of a potato garden that once bloomed. Only traces are left, like old words in everyday speech to remind us of the people that lived there once and the language they spoke.

14
Nora Dan

When the first National School was built below there near the forge, that was 1858, the same year the school was built in Kilgarvan, the old people used to say that when the school was finished it was like a mansion in the middle of all the botháns* that were there that time. My uncle's father-in-law's father claimed that he was the first scholar that ran in the door the morning it was opened, and we have it handed down from him that the schoolmaster didn't know a word of Irish. All you'd hear from him was, 'Ned put his leg in the tub!'

Sayings in English like that were read out of the first book in a very loud chant. The pupils used to stop at the end of every line so that the reading sounded like:

> Ned put his leg in the tub.
> Jack has got a cart and can draw sand.
> In it a horse and hound can run.
> A, n, an. O, x, ox!

The young lad that was sitting alongside my uncle's father-in-law's father, whatever donas* was down on him, when it came to writing he couldn't make the small 'x' of 'ox'. He was one of the Tadhgín Coughlan's east there the road — the family is still there. It was a slate and a slate pencil they used to have for writing, and the schoolmaster went to great pains to show him how to make the small 'x', explaining that it was as simple as putting two small 'cs' back to back. Tadhgín tried it and made a haimes of it. The schoolmaster lost his temper and gave him a thump and the little fellow burst out crying. All the Coughlan's had the bladder very near the eyes! And when small Coughlan saw where the tear fell he began to cry for his bare life, and he said to the schoolmaster:

'Feach anois. Tá an tox báidhte agat!

'You have drowned the ox on me!'

Of course it was an error to say any word of Irish in the class. I'm told in those early National Schools no Irish was allowed, how else could headway be made. The punishment for talking Irish was very severe. There was a tally-rod then, what was known as a bata scóir.* It was about a foot long and a loop of cord was tied at each end of it so that it could loop around a pupil's neck. Then for every word of Irish the pupil spoke during the day there was a notch put on the rod. When they were about to go home in the evening all the notches were counted and for each notch the little Ire-eshan would get a slap of the stick on the open palm. Oh, God help us, all that down on an empty stomach. We're told that it had an effect and the effect was that whatever English was learned off by heart in school remained implanted in the pupil's nut for the rest of his life. The wind had only to rattle the corrugated iron on the cow house at home when my grandmother was off with:

> Tonight will be a stormy night,
> And you to the town must go,
> And take a lantern child
> To guide your father through the snow.

Hardly waiting to draw breath she'd go from Lucey to Lord Ullin's daughter:

> 'Come back, come back,' he cried in grief,
> Across the stormy water,
> 'And I'll forgive your highland chief,
> My daughter, O my daughter!'

In vain the loud waves lashed the shore
Return or aid preventing.
The waters wild went o're his child
And he was left lamenting!

My grandmother loved reciting and was grateful for the gift God gave her —

I thank the goodness and the grace
That on my birth have smiled,
And made me in these Christian days
A happy English child!

That was a big change from what you'd hear a generation before. The poetry they had that time would be recited at night when the people gathered in to the rambling houses. Some poems like Aighneas and Pheacaigh is an Bháis* would be acted out in the kitchen. The 'sinner', by the way at death's door, would lie down on the settle. Then the 'angel of death' would come in and they would recite every second verse, 'the sinner' pleading to be left live on in this valley of tears and 'the angel' trying to coax him away to the flowery meadows of paradise. Another thing they used recite in the houses that time was called An Siota is a mháithair.* That was a recitation for a man and a woman, and my uncle's father-in-law's father said you'd want a fierce actor of a man to play the son. Mother and son would walk around the kitchen, by the way that they were walking along the road, the son headstrong and lazy and she trying to put manners on him. She'd be calling on him to hurry up. 'Téanam ort, téanam ort, téanam ort!' she'd say. 'Come one, come on, come on!'

And he'd be sloping after her, dragging his legs as slow as a snail going to Jerusalem, stopping every now and then to pick blackberries, to smell the flowers or to imitate the birds in the bushes. The poor woman would be worn off the bones trying to make him look lively, and she'd be forever telling him, if he'd mend his ways, of the great rewards that were in store for him when he'd go to heaven. Oh, the lovely picture she painted of paradise! The dry sod always under his foot, a mansion to live in, fiddles always playing and the air thick with archangels flying around!

'Wisha mother,' he'd answer, 'If there's nothing in heaven only angels and music what am I going to fill my belly with?'

My uncle's father-in-law's father couldn't put two words of that poem together for me, but he remembered all the English verses they learned in the National school. As well as committing poems to memory the young scholars had to learn off reams of the catechism. Big rockers of words you could hardly break in a County Council stone-crusher!

Q. What else is forbidden by the sixth commandment?
A. Lascivious looks and touches, idleness and bad
   company; all excesses of eating and drinking and
   whatever may tend to inflame the passions.

God help those small lads. The only thing they ever saw in flames was a furze bush!

All the names of sins they had to learn and sing out at the tops of their voices — Pride, Covetiveness, Lust, Anger, Gluttony, Envy and Sloth. They knew all the deadly sins, more than their parents knew. They knew their transgressions in Irish but they wouldn't know one sin from another in English.

One Sunday Father Bolger lit the altar. He was so vexed about a certain misdemeanour that the people were shivering in their shoes listening to him. When they were coming out the chapel gate after Mass, there was only one word buzzing around in their heads, 'adultery'. Adultery and adultery kept noising in their ears, and they were asking themselves what could it mean! One old woman, Nora Dan, turned to her neighbour, Cáitín the Lady, and whispered to her in Irish, 'Cogar i leith, a Cháit,* what was all this clamper for in the chapel I thought the man'd burst a vein! Or what is adultery?'

'Peaca marfach,' says Cáitín. 'A deadly sin!'

'Oh,' says Nora Dan, a woman that was within a hen's kick of eighty years of age, 'Oh,' says she, 'and how is it done?'

'It is simple enough to do,' Cáitín said, 'the thing is to hold yourself back.'

Cáitín was a great rogue and whispering to Nora Dan she told her, 'That adultery the priest was talking about is nothing more than breaking wind!'

'Oh, sainted hour!' says Nora Dan, 'If breaking wind is a deadly sin I'm going to be roasting in hell for all eternity! What am I going to do?'

And Cáitín the Lady said, 'Go to confession, girl!'

The following Saturday at eleven o'clock Nora Dan belted up to the chapel. Father Bolger, the poor man, had only a nodding acquaintance with Irish, and the penitents going into him didn't know the English names for the sins they were committing, so that the confession box had a great air of comicality about it.

Nora Dan went into the confession box just as Father Bolger was finishing with the sinner at his left hand side and closing the shutter the priest said 'God bless you my child!' to the departing sinner and in a slightly louder voice, 'Say a prayer for me!' Then turning he slid the right hand shutter open and there was Nora Dan flopped down on her knees and she olagoaning her way through the confiteor, 'trí mo choir féin, trí mo choir féin, trí mo mhór choir féin'.* What good was that to Father Bolger when he didn't know what she was saying! So he waited for a gap in the praying and then he said to her, 'What did you do since your last confession?'

Nora said what she had to say, 'Do chommiteas (I committed) adultery, Father!'

The priest couldn't help it . . . I don't know whether he
is supposed to or not, but he looked out through the little
window and when he saw this old woman outside he said,
'How many times?'

'How many time? An mó uair? Oh yes. Once after the
breakfast, father. Twice after the dinner, three times if I
have a big feed or if I bend down. Once after the supper,
father, once before going into bed and once in bed; but,
father, never yet did I commit adultery in my sleep!'

'Are you a married woman?'

'Oh, indeed I am, father and seana* married to Jack
Doran for over fifty years.'

'And your husband . . . does he know that you commit
adultery?'

'No, father. He thinks it's the cat! For you see, father, if I
commit adultery any night in front of the fire, the cat
jumps that high off the flag and drives his two eyes in
through my husband. For you see, father, my husband is
deaf and does not hear the report. Then, presently when
he sniffs the foul atmosphere, the thinks 'tis the cat! So he
takes off his hat and says "Out cat blast you, you dirty
thing you'll stink the house".'

'For your penance say the litany ten nights running
before you go to bed . . . and put out the cat!'

They went the high road and I came the low road, I went
by the bridge and they came by the stepping-stones. They
were lost and I was saved and all I ever got out of my
storytelling was shoes of brown paper and stockings of
thick milk. I only know what I heard, I only heard what
was said and a lot of what was said was lies?

YOUR HUMBLE SERVANT

Introduction

Storytelling is one of mankind's oldest accomplishments. The study of international folktales shows that several of them stretch back in history for thousands of years and are spread over much of the world. We can even talk in some cases of 'megalithic folktales' which still — or until very recent times — fired the imagination of audiences and gave the skilled raconteur the range and material to develop and exercise his prowess. The good storyteller was in many ways a person apart in his community, one whose ability to entertain gained recognition through long experience and who could inspire both awe and humour by the mastery of style and decor. The speaking voice as the medium of adventure forever moving forward, creating a successive tableau of mental pictures joined in a logical — if unreal — structure of events, has for countless generations lightened the everyday cares and sometimes not so commonplace sorrows of people. The story lives on, internally in its shrewd plot-structure and externally in its social and personal attraction. It is the enduring quality which has caused so many writers, philosophers, and psychologists to be indebted to folk tradition.

In more recent times, changes in social structures and life-styles have drastically diminished the vigour of oral storytelling. Even the 'eternal countryman' is becoming an increasingly rarer breed in this age of centralised mass culture. In Ireland, where people have always had a taste for verbal style, the tradition has survived more strongly than in most European countries. An astoundingly rich store of folklore has been collected here in this century, a factor which has made the country a potential world headquarters of folk studies and which sheds light on much of our own history and literature. But the phenomenon of storytelling itself puts forward its claims to recognition in more immediate and homely terms — the power to entertain and evoke dramatic interest. The sense of drama is especially relevant, for the absence of formal theatre in native Irish tradition has meant that much of the dramatic impulse has been assimilated by the oral storyteller and brought to life in his own intrinsic performance. In contemporary society, moreover, storytelling in its specialised forms requires new and more far-reaching media for it to retain its popularity, and the stage is one such medium. It is appropriate, then, that Ireland's best-known storyteller should also be a virtuoso of the theatre. For as long as most of us can remember, Eamon Kelly has been entertaining the people of Ireland and of many other countries with his own very realistic and penetrating brand of storytelling, a brand which is at once authentic to its roots and enlivening in its creative faculties. He is a fine modern example of how tradition can be brought to life by an artist who absorbs it into his own being and reproduces it in a form which crystallises its inherent qualities.

Folklore, when utilised in more formal art forms, often emerges in somewhat gaudy and false-sounding dress, the down-to-earth characterisation lost by an attempt to infuse too much import into its individual elements. In fact, the true folk story depends for its effect on a fine inter-balancing between its composite elements. Eamon Kelly well understands this. His tellings flow aesthetically from within themselves, never delaying too long on a particular aspect to the detriment of others, always carrying forward the narrative through the incidental background information combined with colour and a well-measured sense of humour. Above all, he brings the functional sphere of the stories into his performance. His County Kerry environment comes to life whether he is performing on stage, on radio, on television, or in the more traditional setting of a small group. This sense of locale is at the core of oral storytelling, part of the paradox the other face of which is its universality. The sense of immediacy strikes his audience as it stirs through his regional accent, his facial expressions, his terms of reference, and his flair for sounding echoes deep in the consciousness of his audience. And all this is done in a matter-of-fact manner which is clearly part of the man himself.

No particular storytelling session is exactly like other sessions. On each occasion an atmosphere prevails which is special to that occasion, and the choice of tales told — as well as their sequence and flavour — is part of the entire unit. With Eamon, the storyteller on stage, the audience is fortunate in that the types of narrative involved are ones which he himself excels in — humorous tales and anecdotes in a rural setting. Some of the longer folktales in this selection are found over a wide field in Europe and beyond, and have been popular in Ireland for hundreds of years. Others, as will be clear to the listeners, are less antique and reflect the caustic wit and wishful thinking by which more recent and more true-to-life characters balanced the scales against their less amiable brothers. The humorous anecdote is the most productive form of folklore in contemporary society, and it is thus opportune to hear how this genre is handled by the polished practitioner. Bíonn seacht n-insint ar gach scéal, a deirtear, agus bíodh cluas ghéar againn do na hinsintí is rogha le duine de ríscéalaithe Chiarraí.*

Dr Dáithí Ó hÓgáin
Lecturer in Irish Folklore, UCD

1
Johnny Curtin

There were these two brothers called Devine. Times were bad and they were reduced to working for farmers. Now, they weren't of our persuasion. They were taken on, on trial, at this house and after their first day's work they were given their supper and sent up in the loft to bed. They weren't long above when the woman of the house sent up for them to come down and join in the rosary.

One Devine went down and the other Devine remained above saying, 'that no man should turn his back to the religion he was brought up to.' And when the Devine that went down came up he said to the Devine that remained above, 'We're fixed up in this house for good!'

'How do you make that out?' says he.

'Well,' he said, 'after the prayers the woman of the house put her two hands together and lifting her eyes to heaven she said, "May the Divine assistance remain always with us!".'

Storytelling is said to be unlucky in the daytime — it interferes with the work, except for fishermen while they're waiting to pull in the nets. 'Storytelling,' the biggest farmer in this parish told his servants when he caught them listening to a seanchaidhe* the day of the thrashing . . . 'Storytelling,' he said, 'is a nocturnal pursuit!' And so it ever was. When people collected into a rambling house after a day's work, 'Be telling!' was as common a salute as fáilte romhat!* and the man without some sort of a story to tell, was as welcome as a drop of holy water in the devil's whiskey.

Johnny Curtin, from over here across the river, was hired by a big farmer over Broadfold way on the north Cork-Limerick border. This was at a time when a farmer's wealth was measured by the number of boys and girls he'd have in service. Those servants worked hard for little pay and as the year wore on they all looked forward to coming home on Christmas Eve with their wages in their pockets.

Now the farmer Johnny was hired with was so miserly that he kept Johnny working all that day. It was nightfall before he paid him and let him go, so that Johnny had the dark with him on that long road home. No friendly Christmas candles in the windows to light him on his way, for the houses are few and far between in that quarter.

He had lost all track of the number of times he had gone astray, when coming up to midnight he heard a troop of horsemen behind him. They drew up, and Lord save us! Johnny knew they weren't of this world, for there in the middle of them he saw his aunt's husband that died the year before! They grouped themselves in a half circle around Johnny and told him to sit down. There was a nice low mossy bank at the side of the road. Johnny did.

'Be telling!' the Captain said to him — even fairies were avid for stories at that time!

'I have no story to tell,' says Johnny.

They couldn't believe it that a grown man'd be out that hour of the night agus gan focal in a phluic aige,* and they moved towards him in a very threatening fashion. The captain held them back.

'All right,' he said, 'let him go this time; he's young. But,' says he, 'maybe he'll have a story to tell before morning! What's your name?'

Johnny told him he was a boy of the Curtin's from the parish of Killaha in the diocese of Ardfert and Aghadoe!

'Come on away with us,' says the Captain, 'and we'll have you home in no time!'

'How could I keep up to ye?' says Johnny, 'and ye all on horseback!'

The Captain told him to pull a geosadán, a withered stalk of ragweed, that was at the side of the road. Johnny did and the Captain looking at it said, 'Gruaig ar do cheann, solus i do shúile agus fiachla id' bheal,* and the same to you Johnny if you're ever caught short.' And looking at the geosadán again the Captain said, 'Feoil agus cnámha ort, cosa agus crúba fút, is earbal taobh thiar,* and the same to you Johnny if you are ever caught short.'

Johnny didn't say anything. He wasn't too sure about the crúba and the earbal taobh thiar!

Then the Captain hit the geosadán a tap of a kippen and turned it into a bull calf!

'Sit up on his back now!' the Captain told Johnny, 'But,' he warned him, 'don't open your mouth while you're on his back or it'll be worse for you!'

Johnny hopped up on the calf's back and off they went. Such quilting down through Newmarket and Kanturk, hither through Cuileann Uí Chaoimh and Nohaval Daly, and over the bounds into Rathmore, keeping to the road all the way until they came there to Knockanes School, the horsemen cut left down through Coracow for Killaha — Johnny could see the Christmas candle lighting in his own window! When they came to the Flesk River, there was no bridge there, the horsemen cleared the river and landed in the inch at the other side, and coming up Johnny was thinking in his own mind would the calf have it in him to do it?

They came up to the bank and the calf made one bounce and as he was sailing across the river, Johnny, full of admiration shouted out: 'Say what ye like, that's one hell of a jump for a calf!'

He looked down and there was nothing under him but the geosadán. He fell splash into the river. When he was struggling out the other side in a lipín báite,* the Captain came over an said, 'Have you your wages, Johnny?'

'I have,' says Johnny.

'And what else have you?'

'I have a story now,' says Johnny, 'but who in the hell'll believe it!'

Johnny was a sweet tulip . . . a prime boyo! He told me that he was out in service before he was confirmed. 'We were a big family, there were ten of us there at the time,' he said. 'Two sets of twins! My father was not too strong. He had to be helped in and out of bed. Before the wedding neighbours told my father that he was too delicate for marriage. They did everything they could to discourage him. They even went as far as to get the parish priest to advise him against taking the plunge. "Don't do it," the priest said. "It might prove fatal!"

' "She'll have to take her chance, father!" my old fellow told him.

'But you can't take the book by the cover, small Jerry was only eleven months old when the second set of twins arrived, so that my mother was nursing three of us at the same time!'

Over near Rathawain Johnny went in service, and the bargain was that he'd be left go to school for a few days a week anyway, until after the bishop came.

'I'd be up with the dawn there,' he said, 'and I'd have the cows brought in from the macha — that's their night quarters, helped with the milking, fed the calves, and I'd have the cows turned out again to their day pasture before I'd go to school.

'Con Regan was the man's name I was hired with. Yerra, he had only a small way of living as far as I can remember — he was only going under ten cows. It took me a while to learn the milking. I started stripping, which can be done with the one hand into a small vessel. This is the final draining from the cow, and a rich drop, known as an braoinín snuga; a sup of that into a hot cup of chaw, and a couple spoons of sugar in it and there's no better tonic!

'The first milking was strained and put in low keelers on the stellan* in the dairy, left to settle, and when the cream rose to the top, it was skimmed off with a timber affair like a saucer, and put in a special tub to await the weekly churning.

'Con's kitchen was newly lofted with a stairs going up in the middle. It was meant to have two rooms overhead but the partition wasn't put up yet, the grant run out I suppose! My bed was at one side of the stairs opening, and Con's was at the other. Con, of course, was not alone in his. There was his wife, Annie, and a nice, fat, plubby, twelve month old baby. Some nights Con'd get tired of the child in the bed and land him over to me. I don't know how he avoided falling down the opening in the stairs in the dark with the child in his arms. Then the child'd be so upset in the strange bed, and I'd be so taken up consoling him, that the house could fall down around me and I wouldn't know what was happening!

'When Con's brother called, he was a drover for the Kerrisk's, and Con's house was the first port of call on his journey driving cattle from Molahiff fair up the country. The cattle were put up in the lime-kiln field, and I often wished Con's brother slept there too. But no, he was given my bed, which was only a narrow gauge, so that I had to go in with Con, Annie and the child. Con's bed was huge; you could turn a train in it!

'The first time the proposition was put to me to go in with Con, Annie and the child, I wanted to run away home. I said I'd sleep on the floor, in the hayshed, any-where! It was no use. There was a bolster put at the bottom of Con's bed, I got in first and Annie and the child got in at the top. Then Con and the brother appeared up the well of the stairs. They had the butt of a lighting candle which was quenched while they were preparing for the hammock. Modesty! There was little preparation needed, only walk out of the clothes, everything except the shirt, and dive into bed. And to my dying day I'll never forget when Con stretched his long legs down. The feet emerged at the right side of my head, or was it the left? I forget! I couldn't see 'em in the dark but I knew they were there!

'But I saw 'em in the morning the minute the dawn hit the skylight. They were the most enormous pair of feet I ever saw. Spágs!* The soles of 'em all lumps and welts! I couldn't see the heels as they were sunk into the tick. The toe nails were so long, you'd say it would be no bother to Con to go up the face of Mount Everest without ever spiking the rock!

'Annie must be the shortest piece of a woman in Christendom, for even when I stretched down my feet — and a thing you'd be lazy to do in a like situation — I couldn't find her. But she must be there all right for Con turning, half in his sleep at dawn, I could see his heels now, began whispering to her. His own little birdie he was calling her, and do you know you'd rather be anywhere else at that minute. "Bí ciúin, Con!"* says she, demurring. "You'll wake 'em all up!"

'This made Con cross and he gave me a nudge of his foot and said, "Wouldn't it be time for you to get up and put down the fire. God almighty, when'll you have the cows into the stall? . . . today is Tuesday, tomorrow Wednesday, the day after Thursday . . . the week is gone and nothing done."

'He called the brother then, very cross with him too. When we were dressed and going down the stairs, "Here, catch," says Con throwing me the child, "put him standing into the tay-chest below!"

'I did and gave him a big spoon to be hitting the sides of it. Myself and Con's brother raked the kindling out of the gríosach* and made down the fire. We filled the kettle and hung it on. We went out then and did the choring around

the yard . . . let out the hens, the ducks and the geese.
When we came back in the kettle was singing over the fire,
and Con was coming down   the stairs and he was singing
too!'

2

The Hiring Fairs

Go deo, deo arís ní raghad go Caiseal,
Ag díol is ag reic mo shláinte;
Ag margadh na saoirse im' shuí cois balla
Im' scaoinse ar leath taoibh sráide.
Bodairí na tíre ag teacht ar a gcapall,
Ag iarraidh a bhfuilim hyreálta.
O teanam chun suibháil tá an cúrsa fada,
Seo ar siúl an spailpín fánach! * (see p.139)

Bhí na cursaí fada go leor ag na spailpíní fadó.* Servants
walked a long way to the hiring-fairs. In later years these
fairs used to be held on Sunday after late Mass in places
like Tralee, Mallow, Ennis and Galway. The men'd be lined
up there. They'd have spades if they were going on
harvest work, digging potatoes; or pikes or scythes if they
were going saving hay or cutting the corn. But in January
or February they'd have only the Sunday suit and a bundle
with their working clothes on their backs. An puc ar a
dhrom aige agus é ag imeacht mar a dúirt na sean daoine.*

Looking back, in many ways those fairs were like the
slave markets you'd hear about out foreign. And 'sclábhaí'
which is our word for labourer means slave. The farmers'd
vet the men, you'd think they were buying an animal.

'Walk up there now! Can you milk? Can you plough?
Can you mow? . . . can you follow horses at all? Answer
me this and answer me no more. When is it too late for me
to put down seed potatoes?'

'It is too late, sir, when you can no longer see out through
the branches of an ash tree!'

'Good, good! A very good answer!'

Then the bargaining would start and there would be great rivalry between the rich farmers for a big loose-limbed man, or a fine scopy woman. Those servants would get anything from nine to twelve pounds . . . a year! They'd be fed and found for that, and of course the girls wouldn't get near as much. After the First World War wages went up to twenty and twenty-five pounds, and one man told me he got thirty-one pounds the year of the Eucharistic Congress — whenever that was? But like all the servants at the time, he had to give two weeks, when the year was up, working for nothing. This was known as a tuille.* And he told me too that the woman of that house was related to his mother, and that it was the hardest house he ever worked in.

'And God knows, Ned Kelly,' he said, 'I worked in hard houses in my time. I slept in the stall under the cow's head, and I was glad of her breath to keep me warm in the frost! But that woman was so tight she nearly starved me. Often, late at night, I'd come into the kitchen in my stockinged feet and look for a cake of bread. If there was a piece taken off it I'd take another piece. I'd bring it out to the cúl lochta* over the dairy where I was sleeping, and with my head under the clothes I'd eat it. And even though I was a grown man at the time, I'm ashamed to say it now, many is the time the hot tears came into my eyes at the hardness of that woman. And do you know what I'm going to tell you. She found the bread crumbs in the bed and I never found the cake after wherever she hid it!

'Isn't greed a fright! And what good did it do 'em. Look at Damer the miser. Damer wore out the backside of his trousers sitting on a chair admiring his gold. He was too miserly to buy a new trousers so he sent out for the tailor to put a new seat in his pants. Of course Damer had to go up to bed while the tailor was at it. When the job was done the tailor threw the trousers up to Damer. He put it on and came down and said to the tailor, "What do I owe you?"

'"Yerra, nothing at all," says the tailor, "if you'll let me look at your gold for a while."

'The door was unlocked and a chair brought into the treasury and the tailor sat down admiring the gold. After a while he got up to go.

'"Well," says Damer, "what good did that do you looking at it?"

'"The same good as it is doing you," says the tailor. "Sure all you are doing is looking at it!"'

But before you can look at the gold you must make it first. There was a farmer from near Cloundrohid and he hired a servant in the city of Cork thinking that he might be a better bargain than a country lad. It was late at night when they left the city. The darkest and the coldest night that ever came. The two of them sat into the horse car and drove out into the country. The young lad from the city never saw so much darkness before. On they went, mile after mile, around turn after turn, over humpy bridge after humpy bridge, so that you couldn't blame the young lad from the city for saying in his own mind, 'Isn't it a long way from home some people live!'

When they got to the farmer's house, late and all as it was, the young lad was put to work right away, choring around the kitchen and the yard. After about an hour he was given a cup of cold milk and sent up in the loft to bed. He had hardly the impression of his body made in the feather tick when he was called again to go out and tackle the horse. The farmer was going to Macroom fair to buy a bull calf. He came down and he was given the horse's winkers, and out he went slipping and falling all over the icy yard. His fingers were so numb he couldn't get the bridle on the animal. And the farmer impatient in the kitchen called out, 'What's delaying you?'

'I can't,' he said, 'I can't get that thing back over his head. His ears are frozen!'

He was tackling the bull!

3
The Young Woman's Denial

Oh, her eyes shone like diamonds
You'd think she was queen of the land,
With her hair thrown over her shoulder,
Tied up with a black ribbon band.

There was this young woman and she was going with a young man. After a time they made up their minds to make a match of it, and she swore by all the mysteries of creation since the first star began to shine that she wouldn't marry any other man but him. That was fine until another young man began to take notice of her. They talked, and they walked and in no time they were going together strong, for she found that she had more meas* on him than she had on the first one.

Everything was being settled up for their marriage, but when her first lover heard this, he came to her in the night, just as she was going to bed, and he said, come what will, he would spend that night with her anyway. She said fine, but would he let her be for a short space; that she had forgotten to rake the fire and that she'd run down and do it, as it would be a fright if there was no seed in the morning! He said, all right.

When she went down, instead of raking the fire, she took a shawl or whatever was next to her hand, and went out into the night. She ran for she knew that before long he'd be after her. I don't know why she didn't go towards the man she was going to marry, but she didn't. She kept going until she lost all sense of direction. At last she saw a house and she went in. There was a very respectable man sitting inside by the fire. He was surprised to see her at that hour of the night, shivering with cold and terror. She explained to him what happened.

'You'll be safe here,' he said, 'and you can remain as long as you want. Why don't you come in service to me and I'll pay you well.'

She put up there and did everything that had to be done. He was always in the house during the day, but as soon ever as the night would come, he'd straighten out. She never heard him coming back, and she thought it must be late for he was never in any hurry out of the bed in the morning. He was like this, going out every night and she got it into her head that she'd like to find out where he was going and what it was he was doing.

This moonlight night she followed him and he never suspected that she was behind him. She often wished after that she had never done it, for where did he go but into the graveyard. He went over the stile, and she thought to herself that maybe it was a nearway he was taking, but on looking in through the bars of the gate, she saw him remove a stone flag and disappear into the inside of a tomb! The Lord save us! When she saw this she got very frightened and she ran as hard as she could to the house. In her hurry she lost one of her shoes and when he was coming home after he found it. She heard him coming in that night for he came to where she was, but she let on to be asleep. In the morning, he asked her, 'Where's that other shoe I saw you wearing yesterday?'

'I lost it,' she said, 'when I was giving the milk to the calves.'

'Get that shoe,' he said, 'for your own good get it. Have it here for me tomorrow!'

He went out again that night, whatever time he came home, and in the morning he wanted to know whether she had found the shoe.

'I lost it the day before yesterday,' she told him 'when I was feeding the calves in the haggard behind the house.'

'It would be better for you now,' he said, 'to tell me the exact place you lost that shoe. Have it there for me tomorrow morning or it'll be the price of you. I'll knock the head off you!'

When night came he went out but when he came home she wasn't there before him. She was too frightened to stay in that house any longer. She said she'd look for some place to go in service, some place where he'd never find her. She walked all through the night and in the morning when the sun began to shine, she came to a fine house in an opening between the trees, and she settled there in service, and if she did she was well thought of there, for she was a willing worker. She was a young woman who could turn her hand to any sort of a job she'd be called on to do within the four walls of a house. She was pleasant and witty too and the young man of the house was very taken with her, and he swore that she was the only one for him. When she heard that, she spoke to the priest that was living near them. All the arrangements were made. They were married and in three spaces of time she had a young son.

About twelve o'clock that night, when the old women who were supposed to be minding her fell asleep, the door opened and in came her former master and without raising his voice in case he'd wake the women, he said, 'Where did you lose that shoe?'

'I told you before,' she said, 'I lost it when I was going feeding the calves.'

'If you don't tell me where you lost your shoe,' he said, 'I'll take the child from your side. Do you hear me?'

'But what can I do,' she said, 'that's where I lost it.'

He took the child and walked out and it was her crying, her loud crying, that woke the women. They found the child was gone and they called her husband. His first words were, 'Is she all right herself? We'll get over the loss of the child some way if she is all right!'

It so happened at the end of another year, there was a second child born to the young woman, and the same company of women was sitting up attending to herself and the child that night. And the man of the house was so divarted with his little son that he gave the women a tomhaisín* or maybe two tomhaisíns to celebrate. In the night they fell asleep and again the door opened and in walked the same man.

'You know the information I am looking for,' he said.

'Only too well,' she told him, 'and my answer is the same. I remember well losing that shoe when I was going to feed the calves!'

'Tell me this minute exactly where,' he said, 'or you'll lose your child!'

'Ná tóg mo leanbh uaim! Don't take my child from me. I'll tell you the exact place.'

But when she tried to say it the words wouldn't come to her, because the image of what she saw in the graveyard that night came into her mind, and all she could do was repeat what she had said before, 'I lost that shoe when I was bringing the milk down to feed the calves.'

He took her child and he went away.

The story went out that the child was gone, the husband was called and a lady that was in the house that night said to him, 'If you had married my daughter as everyone wanted you to do, you'd have a wife and a family now!'

'I can't believe,' he said, 'that the woman I married would do anything wrong. I'll pay no heed to what people are saying. I'll wait, and maybe time will tell.'

Time went on, and as happened before, another son was born to her, and as happened before, when the old women dozed off that night, the same man came in and when she didn't give him the answer he wanted, not alone did he take her child but he smeared . . . like chicken's blood he had brought with him on her face and hands and spilled it on the bed and went away.

God help her! She was finished now. Even her husband
that was constant for so long had to give in. The law was
put in motion and what chance did she have? Who was to
give evidence on her behalf? She was tried for doing away
with her children. Sentences were stiff at the time and the
sentence in her case was the rope. The scaffold was erected
outside as was the custom of the time and just when the
hangman was about to put the blindfold over her head, a
coach drew up and in it she saw the man who was the
cause of all her misfortune.

'That woman is innocent!' he shouted out, 'and I'll
prove it!'

He opened the door of the carriage and out came her
two eldest sons, the small one he had in his arms. He came
up and she could see that he was a different man now, the
cloud had lifted from his face.

'I was under a spell,' he told her as he gave her the little
child, 'a black curse. I was condemned to lie down with
the dead every night of my life, and there was nothing
could save me but an innocent person's denial even in the
face of death. You did that for me and I'm a free man now.'
And putting a purse of gold sovereigns into the child's
lap, he went into his carriage and drove away.

When it was gone her husband came over to her side.

'I failed you,' he said, 'when you most needed the support of a comrade. I failed you!' And kicking the toe-cap of
his shoe into the ground to keep down the tulc* rising in
his throat, he said, 'We'll only have to try and make the
best of it.'

She didn't say anything. She took the three children and
went into the house after him. What could she do only
make the best of it!

4
Two Fierce Lies

Men coming home from service were every bit as good as the returned yanks for boasting. Nothing we had at home could match what they had up the country. The land in Limerick was so good, we were told, that if you dropped a spancel in the field after milking in the evening, you'd never find it in the morning the grass'd have grown so high overnight.

And we thought the midges were bad down here, but it seems you could be eaten alive by the breed of midges they had in Tipperary. There was a man there and he had a prize cow, a valuable animal. She had won several cups, and when she had her calf, he kept them together in a wooded place near the river. And he put a bell on her so that the calf would know where his mother was if he strayed through the trees.

Now August is the worst month for midges, they'd eat you without salt if there's no puff blowing. And this way of a heavy evening the farmer heard the bell clanging as if the cow was in trouble. He sent down the servant boy and what was it? The midges had eaten the cow alive! Those midges were massive! And when they had her flesh picked to the bones, they were still so hungry that they took the bell off the cow's neck and rang it for the calf!

> You sporting young blades of Kerry
> A warning take from me!
> Beware of those ticklesome damsels
> You'd meet inside in Tralee.
> They'd fill you with whiskey and porter,
> Till you wouldn't be able to stand,

And before you know what they're after
You are bound for Van Diemen's land

The biggest lie I ever heard used to be told to the tourists by the Killarney boatmen, when those visitors'd ask a contrary question like: 'How deep is the Puch Bowl?'

The Devil's Punch Bowl, as we all know from our geography lesson, is at the top of Mangerton, which overlooks the town and the lakes, and we were told by the master, the few days I was at school, that the Punch Bowl is an extinct volcano the crater now filled up to the top with the purest of spring water. But how deep is it?

'Well,' the boatman used to say, 'there was a Sweeney man up there on the verge of the crater looking for sheep and he fell into it. Down with him and the Lord save us, as it got dark he saw this enormous fish coming towards him, his eyes blazing like the headlamps of a train coming through a tunnel. The fish opened his mouth and Sweeney went down into his belly. That gave him a breathing space! He sat down and lit the pipe' — tourists'd lap that up! 'He looked around and there was the dog, Sooner! — he had followed him down! With that the fish turned tail and instead of going up towards Killarney and civilisation, he was going down into the bowels of the earth.

'"I'll have to get out!" says Sweeney. So he climbed up into the inside of the fish's neck. God knows then, that was a slippery enough track too! He had the strong shoes on, and between that and smoking the pipe and the dog barking and wagging his tail, the fish got very tickly in his throat, he began coughing and coughed them up, and as he came out, Sweeney blew the pipe smoke into the fish's eyes which delayed him. Sweeney kept going out before the fish, holding on to the dog's tail and did that dog make speed! I don't know how many days and nights they were travelling when all of a sudden the water got roasting hot with a bright light shining through it.

'"O God," says he, "we're facing into hell!"

'Not at all. The next thing was they were catapulted into the open air, landing up on a mossy bank. Sweeney shook the water out of his eyes, looked around him, and there he saw this huge animal with a jennet's head on him, sitting on his bottom like a dog begging. He had two short lops for front legs and a young one looking out of his waist coat pocket!

'"Ah, blast it," says Sweeney, "I know where I am now!"

'So he went down the road, got the bus into Sydney and wired home for a change of clothes! And the dog? That dog was crossed with a bush dingo and that's how sheep-dogs came to Australia!'

5

Small Michael and the Major

On your way down from the county bounds, and before
you come to Derrynafinna you'll notice the remains of a
house, that way, in to your left, and at one time there was a
couple living there. An only son was all they had, Small
Michael, and his father died when Small Michael was thirteen years of age and he was left with the mother to
support.

This way coming up to the fall of the year, Small
Michael got a spade and he told his mother that he was
hitting for the harvest hiring-fair in Mallow to try to get a
few pounds together so that they could have some sort of
a Christmas of it.

So he struck out by the side of the Paps, down the
Slugedal and into Millstreet. For all the world it was a fair
day there and a farmer seeing Michael with the spade on
his shoulder, and he so young and so small, for the fun of
it more than anything else, asked him what he'd charge for
a week's work.

'Fifteen bob,' says Michael.

'All that money,' says the farmer, 'and you without a rib
of hair on your face!'

'If it's hair you want,' says Michael, 'why don't you go
and hire a goat!'

Michael met some of the local lads at the fair, they used
to go from here to Millstreet at the time, and he knocked
around with them for the day, so that he was carrying the
night with him when he hit the road again for Mallow.

He was going along until he saw an old man leaning
over a half door.

'Where's you journey?' says the old man.

Michael told him.

'Erra, leave that alone until morning,' he said, 'stick the spade there and come on away in!'

Michael went in. There wasn't any great slacht* on the house. There was no fire down.

'I'm only in from the fair,' the old man said, and stooping under the bed he brought out two coarse bags and throwing one of them to Michael, he said, 'Here, we might as well bring in a night's firing!'

'Twas very dark now, and it struck Michael as strange that the rick of turf should be so far away from the house. He didn't say anything. They emptied the turf out.

'Bad manners to it for a story,' says the old man, 'I forgot to bring in enough potatoes to tide me over till Sunday. Come on!'

So they went off with the two sacks, and if the rick of turf was a good bit away from the house, the potato pit seemed to be in the next parish. The old man took the straw from the mouth of the pit and when his sack was full a dog began to bark.

'Lift this on my back,' he said to Michael, 'I'll be off! You can fill you own!'

Michael had the bag just about full when he was caught by the collar of the coat and lifted off the ground.

'I'm a long time watching to catch you!' says the farmer, frog marching him up to the house. 'Hold him down there!' he said to one of his sons, 'while I'm tackling the horse to bring him into Millstreet.'

He was taken in to the old police station in Millstreet and he got free lodgings there until the court day. When the case was called, Michael told the bench the story as I have told it to you. Maybe times have changed since but at that time poor people were not believed in court, and he got a month in Cork jail. The food wasn't very good there then, and if Michael was small going in, the skin of a gooseberry would make a night-cap for him coming out.

Twenty-six days I think is all that's in a jail month so on the evening of the twenty-sixth day he was put outside the gate and late and all as it was, he belted out the Western Road. 'Twas dark by the time he got to Coachford. He travelled on until he got tired. Then he saw a light in from the road. He went up. There were two doors. He opened one of them and he was in the dairy. He felt around and found a pan of milk on the stellan.* He put his head in that and when he had enough he lay down and went asleep.

He woke in the morning to hear a lot of activity in the yard and he said to himself, 'If I'm caught here now it'll be another free trip to Cork.' He looked around for some place to hide. There was a big dash-churn in the corner. He hopped into it and squeezed himself down. In came a woman and her son. What a day he picked to be coming from Cork jail — it was churning day! They lifted up an enormous tub of cream and spilled it in on top of Michael. She picked up the staff and with the first crack Michael got of it on the nut he rose up with a roar, knocked over the churn and ran out the door.

The woman and her son set two ferocious dogs on him and Michael knew by the cut of them that they'd tear him to pieces, so he threw them the cap and they began licking the cream off it. That didn't delay them long so he threw them the coat and in like manner the waistcoat and the shirt. In the latter end to save his life he had to throw them the trousers. A lot of cream had collected in the backside of the trousers which gave him enough time to cross a small river and throw the dogs off the scent. There he was now as naked as when he came into the world only a lot whiter!

He crept along by the shade of the ditches until he came to a house where there was some washing out, and the hedge, thank God, was a good bit down from the front door. He didn't have much time to pick and choose. The first thing to his hand was a combination, the old men used to wear them long ago. They were a one-piece under suit, long drawers and vest buttoned up to the chin. It was miles too big for him, but by rolling up the legs and the sleeves he was able to move around in it. Then on examining himself he saw that it was no uniform in which to face the public! So he went into a graveyard nearby to hide, hoping there would be no funeral that day and waited for the night to go home.

It was barely dusk when he heard three men approaching and whatever came over him, he called out to them. If he had kept his mouth shut they'd have thought he'd just risen from the dead and ran away.

'God above!' they said, 'you put the heart crossways in us. We thought you were the Major!'

They explained to him that there was this Major in that locality that died a few days ago, a man that had spent years out foreign and picked up some strange religion in Mesapotamia. They said he had a special tomb built for himself . . . he wasn't going to get his feet wet! And he left an instruction that food and everything was to be put in with him, and enough money to get him across the Jordan.

'And as you know well,' they were all looking at him in the drawers, 'as you know well, that's a trip that'll never materialise. The money'll rot down there with him!'

There was only a small opening in the tomb. They un-did the bolt and opened the little door and as they were all too big to go through it, they shoved Michael in and gave him a box of matches. He cracked a match and thunder and turf, there was the coffin on its end with a glass front, and the Major standing up inside in it, and a white coat on him and a white figario* on his head.

He was so frightened he darted out through the hole, but they shoved him back in again for the money. He cracked another match and there was a table and chair there and he came to a box. There was some abhdhar* of money in it, so he handed it out to them, and the dirty ruffians, what did they do? Shut and bolted the door and left him inside!

Poor Michael! He was in a nice pucker now! The first thought that came into his head was how long would the matches hold? For he knew he would die with terror if he was left alone with the corpse in the dark. He cracked another match and dang it if he didn't find a candle. He lit it and sat down on the chair. There was food there, a cake of bread, 'twas all right too for a hungry man, and a bottle of Paddy with a map of Ireland on the label. When he examined the label he jumped out of the chair with fright. The whiskey was down as far as Athone! Was the Major fond of his drop? Was he tippling?

He looked at the box again where he got the money and there written on it was: 'For the first part of the journey.'

That put him thinking and looking around he saw, in a cabúis* in the wall, another box and written on that was, 'For the final stages!'

This was to put the Major into orbit! He opened that and there was any amount of money inside — notes of all denominations. He stuffed them down the leg of his combination, tying his shoelace at the bottom. With that he heard voices outside. He listened, a different crowd — the Major and his money were popular tonight! When they opened the door Michael shot out! And when they saw him in his white underwear!

'The Major,' they shouted. Two of them scattered and the small fellow fainted! Michael took the coat and trousers off him, put them on himself and hit for home, and when he landed into the mother at Derrynafinna, she said: 'Michael, how did you get on up the country?'

'Famous, mother,' he said, 'the men that hired me worked late but they paid me well!' And he threw the roll of notes on the table.

'Buy a bicycle,' she said.

He did. And himself and his mother had one whale of a Christmas of it! They had whiskey hot and cold, porter natural and mulled, ling and white sauce, jelly and tapioca and a roast pig running around with a big knife sticking out of his back and he shouting, 'Eat me! Eat me! Eat me! I'll be gone cold in a minute!'

6

The Bicycle

Rye made bread will do you good,
And barley bread do you no harm,
Wheaten bread will sweeten your blood,
And oaten bread will strengthen your arm.

Before the scythe corn was cut with a reaping hook, and God knows a slow enough process it was too, you'd cut a handful and put it down and so on until you had the makings of a sheaf. But the straw to my mind was better for thatching . . . the blades weren't crushed or broken, moreover if you threshed, or as they said, scutched, the sheaf on the back of a chair sloped against the table, or on the rungs of a ladder, you had nice clean strands to make a súgán* rope to seat a chair or tie down a meadow cock.

The first scythe to come into this corner of the universe was brought from Cork by a young man who was at the butter market. His father was cutting corn with the reaping hook when he arrived into the field with the scythe.

'Shove back there from me, Da,' he said, 'till you see this machine working! But first I'll have to edge her.'

And as we all know the edge is the secret of a good mower. So he took the scythe-board, with the carburundum at the two sides, off the scythe-tree. Then resting the tip of the blade on the ground, he began to rub the scythe-board with a nice circular motion to the two sides of the cutting edge singing as he worked —

> *Some say the devil is dead,*
> *The devil is dead, the devil is dead,*
> *Some say the devil is dead,*
> *And buried in Killarney.*

Then putting his back to the scythe-tree, the blade forward over his felt shoulder and with his left hand on the flange of the blade to firm it, with the same circular motion of the scythe-board he sharpened the tip —

> *More say he rose again,*
> *Rose again, rose again,*
> *More say he rose again*
> *And listed in the army!*

That done he put the scythe-board back on the scythe-tree and taking a grip on the two handles, duirníns as he called them, he settled himself for mowing. The swish of the sharp blade through the corn stems made a sweet sound as he cut a swath the width of the track of a horse car through the field. And if you saw the nice way, with a small motion of the tip of the blade, he could throw all the ears of corn together. Then he halted and turning to his father he said, 'What do you think of that now, Da?'

The old man looked at the cut corn and then he looked at the scythe.

'No word of a lie,' he said, 'but it was an idle man that thought of it!'

And wasn't that old lad before his time! Look at all the idle men we have today because of inventions. After the scythe came the horse-drawn mowing machine. Then the tractor was invented so that even the horses were idle!

There was something new out every week that time and some people wouldn't hear of the new thing until it was standing in front of them! And did it cause some excitement! Jerry Con Rua was over here at the forge the day he saw his first bicycle. All the men were taking the legs off one another rushing out of the forge as the cyclist came down from Casey's Cross, hopping off the road on his solid tyres.

'What is it called?' says Jerry, 'what is that contraption called?'

'A bicycle!' he was told.

'A bicycle. Good!' says Jerry. 'That's the first question the woman'll ask me when I'll tell her about it; "What's it called, Jerry?" Corp an Diabhail* but I have the answer for her now. A bicycle!'

He came home and Juiloo, 'the woman' as he called her, gave him a cup of beef tea on the backless chair sitting near the fire. The comfort some men had that time!

'Any news from the forge, Jerry?' says she.

'Juiloo!' he said, 'you missed it you weren't over at the forge today! A fellow came down the road from Casey's Cross, and as I own to God, he was like he'd be spread legs on the gate of the haggard outside! There were two wheels under it, and his legs were going around. He was going as fast as a galloping horse and his legs weren't even touching the ground!'

'And what was it called, Jerry?' she said.

'Ah ah, I knew that was the first question you'd ask me. And I have it here for you as round as a hoop. 'Tis called . . . There's a "B" in it!'

'Go out there and give a sop to the cows and it will come to you, Jerry!' she said, consoling him.

He went out and you could see him through the window crossing the yard, a pike of hay over his head, pausing every minute, sops falling down all round him, and he talking away to himself:

'And it wasn't a big word. There's a "b" in it! Whether the "b" is in the back of it or the front of it I don't know! There's a "b" in it. Bad luck to it, there's a "b" in it!'

He was like a bag of weasels all day. No word out of him at the supper. The children had to shut up and the dog had to be put out as they were disturbing his train of thought!

The rosary was brought forward and the trimmings cut, the small lads put up to bed with a strict injunction to be silent. When there was utter quietness in the house he put Juiloo sitting down and implored of her to say all the strange names she heard in her geography lesson, the mountains of Greece and the rivers of China to see would anything give him an inkling. She went through as much ráiméis* as she could — but it was no good. They went to bed. And Juiloo dropped off the second her head hit the bolster. What did she want awake for, and her man preoccupied!

And here was Jerry, his hands behind his head looking up into the darkness searching every nook and cranny of his head for the word wherever it had gone to!

About two o'clock in the morning he sat up and nudging Juiloo he began to shout:

'I have it! I have it!' Juiloo didn't know where she was.

'I have it!' he said.

'What have you, Jerry?' she said, all concern.

'I have it!' says he, 'Sickly boy!'

'Mhuire Mháthair!'* says she, 'I hope it isn't contagious!'

7

The Singapore Policeman

One of the Túrnóineach's was coming home after spending ten years in the Singapore police, on a pension of a pound a day. This was at a time when a man'd bring home change out of a shilling after a day's carousing at Barraduv sports. The Singapore policeman had married an English lady while abroad, and she would have to be put up in the house too for a few nights anyway. The house, the ancestral home, was presentable enough and well kept when the mother was alive. The son, the policeman's brother, who was in it now, had the misfortune to marry Hannah Damery. She was pure easy-going, the clothes looked as if they had been thrown on her with a hay fork, sitting on the chair from morning till night chewing away and the children lapadawling* around the floor! That kind of a woman!

Neighbours came in to help her put some slacht* on the house. They whitewashed it inside and out, green rushes were cut and spread on the muddy approaches to the door. Grandma's bed was done up for the strangers, the tick put outside on the hedge to air it. Dust rising out of it as it was beaten with the back of a grubber, the sheets were washed and bleached to knock the flour brand out of them! Crockery was borrowed for the table, and a big feast prepared for the homecoming night. 'Spare nothing,' Hannah said. Thinking of herself she was! All the neighbours were invited, and Hannah said they'd have some of that 'shaky, shivery stuff you'd ate with a spoon'. So jelly and trifle figured largely on the menu. They forgot the hundreds and thousands, little spheres of no consequence as Father Horgan called them at the stations, to shake on the trifle.

But early in the day, Hannah dispatched the husband to town for some, as she said the trifle wouldn't be the thing without them! And whether it was that she didn't give the husband the right description, we don't know, but in the shops in town they didn't seem to get the hang of what he was looking for, so he wound up in a bicycle shop where he purchased a large carton of ball bearings!

When the night came these were shaken on the trifle, and when people took a few spoons of it they found under their teeth what they couldn't chew. And they couldn't very well spit it out! How could they with the English lady and all there, though some did make off the yard to see what the weather was doing. Later in the night and the following morning people suffered dire pains in their lower regions and these two women met at the well out in the day.

'Airiú,* tell me, Mary,' says one, 'did you try any of Hannah Damery's trifle yesterday evening?'

'I did,' says Mary, 'and it is I am the sorry woman. Up and down all night! Himself was going to go for the priest for me! Did it have any effect on you?'

'Effect! Dia linn is Muire!* I thought it was "pintecitis" I was getting. An awful deadness in my right side! Like a lump of lead! And I thought then, with respects to you, I thought if I could break a little wind, that it would bring relief. Well, when I bent down to light the fire I did, and shot the cat.'

8
Padden

There was a time in the history of Ireland, when you couldn't throw a stone without rising a lump on a king's head — they were that plentiful!

At that time, there was this couple, Paddy and Norrie Kirby and they were twenty-one years married and they had no family. They were heart-broken because of it, no one to leave the place to, the grass of a cow and two goats is all they had, but to them that was wealth indeed.

One night on his way home from Killarney, Paddy was passing by the Seven Stoney Sisters — that's the druids' circle there near Lissivigeen — and a grey man came out. He spoke to Paddy, 'Why are you so down and out?' he said. 'Why are you so mournful?'

'Well,' says Paddy, 'I'm hitting up to middle age . . . 'tis all down hill now to the grave, and I have neither chick nor child to cry after me! No son to put a shoulder to my coffin.'

'You mightn't be always like that!' says the grey man.

'Wisha, God help us!' says Paddy, 'I'm married now twenty-one years and there's no likelihood of anything yet!'

'You can take my word for it,' says the grey man, 'that in three spaces of time, your wife Norrie, will present you with a son.'

Paddy went home.

'I'm afraid,' says Norrie when he told her what transpired, 'that *that* grey man is a bit of a rogue!'

'Only time can tell,' says Paddy. 'We might as well go to bed anyway!'

They went to bed, and six months after it was plain to anyone looking at Norrie that an event was expected. When her time came, Paddy was planting a tree in the field oright* the house out, in honour of the occasion, when one of the women ran out to say his son was born! The poor man was so overcome with excitement that the heart gave out, and he died on the spot.

The son was called Padden, a variation of the father's name, and his mother promised him, as soon ever as he could follow what she was saying, that she would keep him on the breast until he'd be big enough and strong enough to pull the tree from the roots that his father planted the day he was born.

When he was seven years old she put him out in the field and told him to pull the tree. And even though he had a pair of arms on him as big as a lad twice his age, he couldn't knock a shake out of the tree. The mother saw that there was nothing for it now but nurse him on for another seven years. This she did and at the end of that time, when he got up he was so big that his head went through the ceiling. He had to crawl on all fours to get out through the door. Once outside he spit on his hands and made for the tree and we must not forget, that all this time the tree was growing too! so he had his work cut out for him. He got a grip on it, and with the first heave the ground shook and cracked — for seven perches all round. He pulled again and you could hear the roots breaking below, and with the third heave, he brought the tree clear out of the ground, leaving a hole big enough to bury all the cows that died of foot-and-mouth disease since the first homing pigeons brought that malady in from the continent of Europe!

He got a saw then and a hatchet and lopped off the branches and the roots, and rounding the butt of it he made a walking cane out of the trunk of the tree.

'Mother,' says he — and she was proud of him! — 'You worked hard to keep me in sustenance for fourteen years. It is time for me now to do something for you. I'm going off to seek my fortune so that you can live in comfort in the remaining years of your life!'

He set out through the country as it was then — no
roads or railways — and never drew rein till he came to
the court of the King of Leinster. And when the King of
Leinster saw this big fostúch* of a man outside the front
door, he came out.

'What are you looking for?' the king said.

'I'm looking for work,' says Padden.

'What can you do?' says the king.

'I can do anything,' says Padden.

'I'll make a bargain with you now,' says the king. 'I'll
give you three jobs to do and if you succeed in doing them,
I'll give you your weight in gold going home, but if you
fail, what you'll get'll knock a hop out of you — cut the
top of the ear down off me!'

'I'll chance my luck anyway,' says Padden. 'What'll I do
first?'

'Go down,' says the king, 'and empty that lake below,
and your dinner will be waiting on the table for you when
you will come up.'

'And where will I put the contents?' says Padden.

'Empty it over that small hill and down into the glen!'

Padden went down and he ran his walking cane, the same
as you'd run the handle of a shovel under a load of sand,
under the hill and made a tunnel level with the lake shore.
He went down then on his two knees and he sucked up the
lake and shot it back through him and into the tunnel and
down into the glen. A cloud-burst, is how the *Cork Examiner*
described it, or whatever *Examiner* was there at the time.
Only goes to show how wrong newspapers can be! A wall of
water came down the valley. People saving hay in the inches
ran for the high ground — didn't go back for their coats!
Only a few men thatching houses is all that were saved.
Even the local tailor that was crossing the stepping stones at
Gortalick at the time was swept away and as he was borne
off on the breast of the flood he was heard to shout, 'Tá rud
amháin cinnte beidh an gleann seo gan táilliúir!'*

When the king saw that Padden had the lake as dry as the palm of your hand, he said to himself, 'This fellow is not the fool I took him to be. If I don't get a harder job for him, I'll soon be parting with my gold.'

'What'll I do now?' says Padden.

'Don't do any more today,' the king said, 'go in and have your dinner!'

That same night, the king went to his adviser, the Dall Glic.* He told him about Padden.

'You'll have to give me a hard job for him to do. Something that's next door to impossible or I'll soon be parting with my money!'

'Haven't you a brother in hell?' says the Dall Glic.

'I have,' the king said. 'There's hardly any other place that blackguard could be.'

'Send Padden down for him. Say that you want to see him!' says the Dall Glic.

The following day the king dispatched Padden down to hell for the brother.

'How'll I know him?' says Padden.

'He'll have only one tooth,' the king said, 'standing up like a golaun* stone in the middle of his lower jaw!'

When Padden began hammering on the gate of hell with the trunk of the tree, the devils inside started shivering in their shoes. They thought it was the end of the world, so they opened the gate.

'I'm here,' says Padden, 'for the King of Leinster's brother!'

'How'll we know him?' says the devils.

'By a single tooth,' says Padden, 'standing up like a golaun* stone in his lower jaw!'

Off with the devils and it isn't one fellow they brought back, but twenty single-toothed, ugly looking devils as look alike as guinea hens.

Padden had no notion of spending time in the hot, sweaty atmosphere of hell, finding out which of these was the king's brother, so he drove them all out before him back to Leinster and into the royal parlour. I can tell you the king got a fright when he saw smoke coming out of the boarded floor where they were standing. In no time at all they burned twenty holes through the floor and fell into the cellar.

'Get 'em out of it,' says the king in a rage, 'before they turn Ireland into an inferno. Drive 'em back down to hell!'

'What about your brother?' says Padden.

'The devil turn him,' says the king, 'if they are an example of what hell can do to a man, I don't want cut, shuffle or deal with him! Drive 'em down!'

While Padden was on his way to hell with the twenty toothless men, the king went again to his adviser. And the Dall Glic said, 'It seems nothing is impossible to Padden and you'll be without your gold!'

The Dall Glic gave the brain a bit of a shaking and then he said: 'Haven't you a deep shaft in the yard where you were mining for copper?'

'I have,' says the king.

'Send Padden down to dry up the bottom of it,' says the Dall Glic. 'And when he's below, get some of your hefty men to throw a heavy weight down on top of him!'

The following day, the king showed Padden the mine shaft. 'And if you can dry up the bottom of it,' says he, 'that'll be the third job done and I'll give you your weight in gold going home and a new hat into the bargain!'

Down with Padden and when he was below, the king got his men to throw a millstone down on top of him, but the hole in the centre of the millstone was the same size as Padden's head and when it landed on him it was such a nice fit he thought it was the new hat!

He dried up the bottom of the shaft, came up and when the king saw him emerging out of the shaft with the millstone on his head, he was man enough to admit defeat, so a huge weighing scales was procured and as Padden made for it the king said to him: 'Surely you're not going to stand on it with your new hat on!'

'Isn't it as natural for me,' says Padden, 'to stand on it with my hat on as with my trousers on!'

The king was done for again and he said, 'All right!' but of course he didn't have enough gold in his kingdom to weigh down Padden, but he gave him what he could afford.

Padden came home to his mother. He dined her and he wined her; he made her burn her old shawl and he bought her a nice navy coat, a big floppy hat, white gloves and the swankiest pair of 'lastic boots you ever clapped eyes on, and when the days lengthened out into spring, he brought her here and there to see the sights. They went everywhere together, to races and regattas, and the last place they were seen was at the hurdygurdies at Puck Fair, the two of 'em going around on the chairaplanes!

9

The Cat and the Splinter

'Tis only when you'd see the big blaze of electric light in the houses at the present time that you'd wonder how the people before us managed with the rush light and the splinter!

The rush was peeled — old people'll follow me here, for if they didn't see it they heard tell of it. The rush was peeled — not fully, a thin strip was left on at the back for reinforcing, otherwise the white core'd go in brus,* in your hand. The peeled rush was dipped in goat's fat, or any other fat, and allowed to harden, and a carn* of them'd be kept in the cúilín* in the corner. Though to my mind the rush was not a permanent light. It didn't give the battle, but 'twas handy for ootumawling* around the house, or showing the old couple to bed.

Then you had the bog deal splinter — a pure dinger!* And that was the only form of illumination you had before the candle, the tilly lamp or Ardnacrusha were ever dreamt of. To select a splinter you'd select a straight-grained creachaill* of bog deal and with the saw you'd run it off into lengths of, say, from one-and-a-half to two feet. Then with the hatchet you'd come at these lengths and cleave them down into thin strips 1½" x ¼" and put them up in the shoulder of the chimney to season for the winter. And at that time, up on the wall you had a bracket — a holder made by the smith, and when night'd come, lob a blazing splinter into the bracket and you'd have plenty of light for playing cards or any other caper.

Earthen or mud floors you had in houses then, except for the flag of the fire, and the gáirdín na nóinín'd* be danced on that flag, or the door would be taken off the hinges to make a platform, and I often heard it said that every member of the company would light a splinter in the fire and ring the musician and the dancers with a ribbon of light. It was lovely! And how long would a splinter live? Half-an-hour, I suppose, maybe longer, according to the quality: but when it'd die, you could light another one, or two, they were plentiful and there was no fear of blowing a fuse!

Well, in the time of the splinters there was this carpenter, and he was living alone in a small house. He had no apprentice or servant, only a butter-coloured cat called Bubble, for he was puffed out like a football. The carpenter was a first-class man, served his time, did journey work, and was in great demand for making common cars, and all that goes with them — wheels, butt, rail, guards and seat across.

In the kitchen he used to function for business was that brisk he had no time to put up a workshop. In the winter he'd be working at night. He'd have the body of a car, we'll say, together on the floor, and he'd be fitting the back set-lock down on the shafts and sidelaces — knacky work! and you'd want good light for it. A splinter is all he had, and 'twasn't the thing, for he'd want it at the car where he'd be fitting, and he'd want it at the bench where he'd be cutting, and he'd want it at the grindstone where he'd be edging, and a man has only two hands, so what did he do but train the cat to hold the light. And if all belonging to you were dead you'd weaken to see the cat holding the splinter out at arm's length, so as not to singe his whiskers!

In the beginning, the carpenter was saying to the cat, 'Down this way, Bubble. Slant it over. Right! A bit more to your left. That's the tack! Hold it there now, that's the real goat's toe!'

And so on 'till the cat got so well up that he knew the carpenter's next move and was there before him. All this was miraculous of course, though I'd say that the cat wasn't in with himself for the ears were only half cocked and the tail was down flat. But there again I could be wrong, no man knows what goes on inside in an animal's head. That's one closed book to us anyway!

Well, news of Bubble and the splinter leaked out. The saddler told the master, the master told the scholars, the scholars told their mothers and the mothers told the parish! And when night fell you couldn't draw a leg in the carpenter's yard with the crowd gaping in the window all marvelling at Alladin. A tay-man came the way. In with him to the carpenter's and when he saw the cat supporting the blazing splinter he was spellbound. When he found his tongue he said to the carpenter, 'How do you account for the animal's perspicacity?'

'Training,' says the carpenter, 'it overcomes nature!'

'I doubt very much,' says the tay-man, 'if there's one atom of truth in that.'

The tay-man went away in his pony and car and when he came back in a week's time, the carpenter was having his supper and there was Bubble sitting on his corragiob* at the top of the table holding the light. The carpenter invited the tay-man to sit over. He did. And the tay-man could see that the carpenter was full of admiration for Bubble, and hopping the ball, he said, 'Perspicacity my eye! No amount of drilling can overcome the natural bent in an animal!'

'There's an animal there now for you,' says the carpenter, 'and nothing will deflect him from his duty!'

'Would you like to bet on that?' says the tay-man.

The carpenter said he would and bets were put down, and the tay-man took out a Van Houeten cocoa tin and taking off the perforated cover he let a mouse go on the table!

The cat dropped the light. Is treise dúchas ná oiliúint!* and went after the mouse. He was the only one of the three of 'em that could see in the dark!

10

The Tay-man

A tay-man put up one night with a man and his wife in a one-roomed house in which there was only one bed. You had a lot of those houses at that time — thatched huts built by the farmers for their workers. They cared about the comfort of their servants! The tay-man put his pony in the boarded shed outside. Indeed he wouldn't have stayed in such a poke of a place at all, only that the night was stormy and he couldn't get to his usual lodgings.

Before they went to bed the woman of the house took up a lovely cream cake . . . oh! the aroma that was from it, and put it standing that way — a wheel with four spokes — on the ledge of the dresser. Well, the tay-man's teeth were swimming inside in his mouth for a bite of the cake, and the wife noticing the hungry look on his face was about to break off a piece for him.

'No, no,' the husband said, 'you'll ruin the cake if you break it while it is hot! Can't he wait until morning like the rest of us?'

They went to bed. The wife next to the wall, the husband next to her, and the tay-man on the outside. God knows then that the bed was narrow enough too, so that they had to lie spoonways, and when one'd turn they'd all have to turn! In the course of the night when the husband had occasion to go out, which was often . . . . he had a little frequency . . . that runs in families! . . . he made the wife go with him. He was slow to let her with the tay-man, and indeed she complained bitterly about having to go out in the yard, the breeze going through her! And as she said herself; moreover when she didn't have occasion to!

In the end she kicked against going out, and the husband, still nervous of leaving her alone with the tay-man, lifted up the cradle with the child in it, and put it between the two of them in the bed and went out. When he came in, after shedding the tear for Parnell, he lifted up the cradle and put it back on the floor — the busy night he had!

Around six in the morning, the storm got so bad it began to rip the boards off the shed, and the husband in his excitement to get out to tie it down, forgot all about the tay-man. When he was gone, the wife turned to the tay-man and said:

'Now is your chance!'

He got up and ate the cake!

11

The Connaughtman's Story

According to Johnny Curtin when his father was putting in for the pension, he couldn't find his age. What happened in a case like that was, you would go before the Old Age Pensioners' Committee. Father Horgan that was at the head of that at the time, and if a man could remember an event, an act of God or such like, that happened long ago, that would be taken as evidence of age, and an affidavit would be sworn to that effect.

Curtin's father, a man who couldn't stop talking once he started, was asked if he remembered the night of the big wind? A usual question when the pension came out in nineteen o eight. He said he did. He was sitting inside by the fire, he said, when the wind blew in the door and that gale was so strong it whipped the roof off the house. Even the pot of potatoes boiling over the fire was taken holus bolus up the chimney, and as it emerged at the top it was struck by lightning . . . you could see the steam rising out of it . . . and they were the first spuds to be boiled by electricity! The pot got as red as a coal of fire and went floating off through the air. The people running out of their houses and seeing the ball of fire in the sky thought it was one of the great astronomical tokens of disaster given down in the prophecies of Saints Moling and Colmcille, when Ireland will be invaded by Spaniards, Portuguese, Turks, French and rattle-snakes: when a clergyman wearing a black cloak will lead the men of the North into the valley of the Black Pig, and fighting men will be so scarce that old lads will be turned in their beds three times to see would they be fit to shoulder a gun! The young will forget what men looked like, and a daughter and her mother crossing Thomond Bridge will see a figure. And the daughter will say, 'What is that?' And the mother will say, 'That's a man!' and the daughter will start laughing and that night the mother will kill the daughter so that she'll have the man for herself!

'Stop, stop, stop!' says Father Horgan, 'do you want to bring the flames of hell jumping up at me. Give him the pension,' says he, 'or we'll be here till doom's day!'

Of course it was in the prophecy too that the time would come in Ireland when we wouldn't know the women from the men . . . the Lord save us! And that the wrapper would be worth more than the contents, though that is said to have come to pass during the Economic War with England when farmers couldn't sell their stock.

Calves were skinned, the hides were sold and the carcasses thrown away. Of course Bull gave in in the end but, like always, he waited until we were nearly all dead!

> *It was in the town of Tralee she first met him,*
> *Coming down from the labour exchange.*
> *He had five shillings dole in his pocket.*
> *And a voucher for nine pounds of beef!*

In bad times like that when the price of what you have to sell is falling and the price of what you have to buy is rising, a small farmer might have to go out in service himself, and leave the place to his wife to work it with whatever help she might get from a neighbour or a relation.

Now, it so happened, away far back, that there was this man living in the province of Connaught. He wasn't long married, a couple of months maybe and he decided, so that they could keep body and soul together, that he would go out in service for twelve months. So he crossed the Shannon and into the rich land and after a long time travelling he was hired by a big landowner and he worked for him for twelve months.

He was treated well, the wages were good, he slept in the house and sat down to the same table as the family, and when a bullock was killed, looking into his plate, you'd see as much beef as turnips. He had time off to go to a football match or pitch and toss, and when Christmas Eve came round the farmer said to him, 'I'd take it as a great favour if you'd stay for another twelve months.'

'I would and willing,' he said, 'if I could get an account to Nora.' She was the wife. There were no roads or railways, no postmen or telegraph wires at the time. 'But Nora is a knowledgeable person,' he said, 'and maybe she'll understand.' So he remained on for another twelve months, and at the end of that time coming up to Christmas Eve the boss called him in.

'You are going now, ' he said, 'and which will you take: three pieces of advice or your wages?'

'You were always fair in your dealings with me,' says the Connaughtman, 'which would you take yourself?'

'I'd take the three pieces of advice,' the farmer said. 'For the road now here are three oaten cakes herself made, a small one, one not so small and a big one, but on no account broach the big cake until you are landed at home!'

'All right,' the servant said as he went out the door.

'Come here. You are going now without the three pieces of advice. Never go the near-way when you are on the road at night. Never sleep in the same house where a young woman is married to an old man and, never make a judgement when you are in a temper!'

So the man from the west set out for home taking a bite out of one of the small cakes when he got hungry and drinking a sup from a well. When night came he fell in with a group of men, who like himself were going home from service with their wages in their pockets. They came to a place where the men said they knew a short-cut through a wood, but he remembering the advice held to the public road. Times were as bad then as they are now, the men were waylaid and robbed of their money.

He went on another while and as he was tired when he came to a house he went in. He was given shelter and the young woman spilled him out a cup of milk. Looking around he could see that there was no other one in the house with her only an old man of perished appearance sitting by the fire. He asked the young woman, 'Is he your husband?' and she said, 'He is. God help me!' And remembering the second piece of advice, Never sleep in the same house where there is a young woman married to an old man, he got up and went out. 'Twas raining now, so he took shelter in a car house.

He wasn't long there when a young man came and tapped on the window. She put her head out: 'All right,' she said without lowering her voice — the old man must be deaf! She came out and he overheard them planning together . . . how to get rid of the old man. He said to himself that it was time to go, so as not to get implicated in that.

He walked on and when he got drowsy he put his back to a rick of hay or a stack of oats and slept for an hour. By the middle of the following day the two small oaten cakes were finished and even though he was often hungry after, he never broached the big cake, and when he landed at his own house that night he put it on the table. Nora, his wife, had great welcome for him. Such a long time! But he said he was so tired after the journey, he'd throw himself on the bed for a while, and made for the room door.

'Oh,' she said, coming before him. 'You can't go up there. John is sleeping in that bed with me.'

'John!'

'Oh,' he said. 'Croí an Diabhail!'* and flaring up he rushed over and caught hold of the tongs and just then he thought of the third piece of advice: Never make a judgement in a temper!

'What's wrong?' says Nora, going into the room. 'Look at John!' she said from inside, 'he hasn't his clothes on him yet!'

When he heard that he was going to go for the tongs in earnest! She came down the room door.

'Hold the child!' says she, 'I'll get the supper. We'll try a piece of the Kildare bread!'

'Twas his own child, a fine agreeable eighteen month's old baby, teeth up and down on him, and called John after his own father!

'Cutcha! Cutcha! Cutcha!' he said, poking his finger at the laughing bundle.

And all the tiredness went out of his bones as he danced around on the flag of the fire. Nora was singing as she laid the table. She broke the cake and what was inside in it? His two years wages! So they put down the kettle and made the tay, and if they didn't live happy that we may!

12
Filling the Firkins

Farmers like to see their servants observing their religious duties, but they wouldn't give them a seat on the side-car going to Mass on Sunday. No! Nor no seat in the family pew the farmer owned in the chapel No, nor no seat at the dinner table in the farmer's house on Sunday nor any other day!

'The servants always had their meals abroad,' Johnny Curtin told me, 'abroad in the back kitchen or the linny. Potatoes figured largely in our diet,' he said . . . 'very filling! But how would you make sure you got your fair share when all the hands would be reaching into the ciseán* of spuds in the middle of the table? Well, I'll tell you, and this is the advice I got leaving home, "Be eating one, be peeling one, have one in the heel of your fist and have your eye on another one!"

'In one place I worked,' Johnny told me, 'the farmer used to come out to the linny and sit with the servants. Then just as we were all reaching for our first mouthful, the farmer would rise to his feet and say: "Grace before meals. In the name of . . . and the Holy Ghost. Amen!"

'Then we'd sit down and start wiring into the golden wonders, and as I own to my sweet adorable and divine God above in heaven tonight, I wouldn't have hardly got to the spud in the heel of my fist, when the farmer was on his feet again saying, "Grace after meals."

'When we had blessed ourselves he'd move back from the table, and we were all so young and so innocent at the time, and God help us, so ill-equipped to fight for our rights, that we'd take our caps and go out the door half hungry. The farmer then'd go into the house and sit down with his wife to his real dinner!

'And what was left of our meal, the potatoes, were broken up into a big tub, given a shake of Indian meal, and a dash of skimmed milk and taken out to the stall-fed animals that were being fattened up for the market.

'But not all men you'd meet,' Johnny told me, 'were like that, but those that were, were bad, and the wives were worse. I was coming into my supper, such as it was, one night. I was in my stocking feet, and the woman of the house, whose back was to me, didn't know I was there, and she said to the husband: "Did you put out the servant boy's cup and did you thin the milk for him?"

'And you'd think the servant girls, that were more in the house with the food under their hands, would fare better than we did. They did not! And you didn't have to go up to Limerick or Tipperary at all to see it. It happened here inside in your own parish.

'When the farmers were joined in butter, you remember that, Ned? Well, their wives would all collect in one house once a week to pack the firkins for dispatch to Cork. The butter'd have to be washed and blended, the servant girl, the two arms dragged out of her, drawing water from the well a couple of fields away; lifting the heavy firkins — all the horse work was hers! When the job was finished there'd be a feast in the parlour. Indeed the servant girl might be sent down to the village for a drop of the foxy boyo. The kettle would be ready, on the boil when she came back to heat the glasses. Then the bottle of whiskey would be tilted into the glasses.

'"Oh, no, no, no," you'd hear the women saying. "That's enough for me! It travels to the head!"

'Boiling water was added, a couple of lumps of loaf sugar and a clove! Oh glory! The sound of the spoons in the glasses. Small bells tinkling!

'Like the parish priest that fell from grace! The bishop was discussing it with the canon at a month's mind. The canon was all concern, for as he remarked it is so seldom a thing like that happens. And he said to the bishop lowering his voice, "Was it punch, my Lord?"

'"Yes," the bishop said, "and Judy!"

'While the women were sipping the punch, the table in the parlour'd be laid by the servant girl. She'd bring in plates of this and that, cream cake and apple tart, and last of all the special china-ware teapot, and the tea-cosy! The women'd sit in — such a babble of talk after the punch. And if the servant girl lingered at the door looking long-ingly at the laden table, the woman of the house would say to her, "Go on away out there. You'll find something to do outside. Standing there, watching every bite that goes into our mouths!"

'The servant girl would go out and all the other ladies would agree with the woman of the house. All talking together, you could hardly make out what they were saying!

'"You're right not to be giving her the habit of it!"

'"She'd ate you out of house and home. The size of her!"

'"Pamper 'em, I always say, pamper servant girls and they'll walk on you!"

'"The next thing is they'll be throwing the glad eye at your son, or, the Lord save us, at your husband maybe!"

'"Oh, the glad eye is no good to the man of this house. John has enough to do as it is. Eh Hanna!"

'"Cut 'em down on the food, that's the thing!"

'"Then they won't have the gimp* on 'em for it!"

'But there was nothing more calculated to drive a farmer and his wife off their rocker than for the servant boy to fall in love with the daughter. I tell you a match'd be made for her in double quick time with a man of substance.'

13
Kate from Baltimore

It is her father Frank I have to thank
  For being in this sad state.
He swore for sure that I was too poor
To go and marry his daughter Kate.
He came to me, 'and young man,' says he.
'Your folly now give o'er,
Or this very night I will have your life
In the town of Baltimore.'

I went to Kate for to relate my misery and woe,
She said to me, 'Oh John!' says she, 'There is no
  release but go.
For if I were you I would go and enlist
  his wrath for to avoid,
And what's more,' says she, 'Oh I long to be
a brave young soldier's bride!'

Away I went and I quite content I joined the 98ths.
I'm enlisted now, but she broke her vow, farewell
  to my love, Kate.
And the note she wrote, Oh my heart nearly broke,
As I read it o'er and o'er
Saying, 'I am married to a man who is a farmer's son
  from near the town of Baltimore!'

14
The Apprenticed Doctor

Up the country where habitations are few and a knocker on every door, I don't know what servants did during the few hours they'd have off at night. Of course, they wouldn't be off in every house. They worked until they went to bed. Around here where farmers were big enough to afford hired help, the servant boy could knock into the rambling house at night in the winter time. Lift the latch and walk right in. This'd be the residence of some honest to God farmer that was pulling the devil by the tail, or the house of the postman, the carpenter or the tailor.

These rambling houses, as far as I remember, were a cross between the Dáil and the Cork Opera House! There you'd have debates, old 'statesmen' would answer questions and try to unravel the mysteries of the universe and the economy. You'd have stories and riddles, songs, music and an occasional dance. In the long summer evenings, the Dáil would adjourn! Go to the country! The company would sit on a mossy bank under a shaped hedge by the roadside, and passers-by could add a note to the general hilarity.

Another place of assembly in the fall of the year was around the mouth of a lime-kiln, the red glow from the fire lighting up the men's faces. At that time every well-to-do farmer had a lime-kiln on his property. It was built against a hill in a leaca.* You'd cut an 'L' shape and clear out that triangle of earth. Then the stone-mason would build the kiln, circular inside, like an upside-down cone or the paper tómhaisín* the old women used to get the snuff in long ago. Only a couple of feet wide at the bottom and widening out as it went up to about six or eight feet in diameter at the top. It would be twelve or fifteen feet high, and had to be built of good heat resisting stone — the end grain to the fire. As the mason went up, like the Gobán Saor building the round tower, he built the front wall, the breast of the kiln, and the two returning walls. The removed earth he would now, return fill and ram, as they say, into the spaces in between.

In the front wall you had the eye of the kiln, arched . . . it would remind you of the eye of a bridge, or a fire place with an opening at the bottom to remove the burnt lime. Now to work it . . . you see, at the top level there was a gap or a gateway where you carried in the raw limestone and the turf with which to burn it. And at the lower level you could back in your horse and car and draw away the burnt lime — 'twas like a human being — in above and out below!

To work it: you started off with a blazing fire, a good few feet of turf, and then a layer of limestone, broken small, another layer of turf and so on, limestone, turf, until it was filled to the top, and then you'd see the men jumping on it to pack it down. As it burned and the turf was reduced to ashes, the lime fell down and more layers were added at the top and this went on for days or weeks until the lime was burned.

There was a fierce draught in that chimney and when the kiln caught fire, in no time it developed such an intense heat that the grey limestone was burned through and whatever chemical was knocked out of it, it emerged below a creamy white and hardly half the weight it went in. Take up a small piece of it and let a few drops of rain fall on it, and it would crumble in your hand dissolving into a fluffy powder. That was used for making mortar and fertilising the land.

In the fall of the year that time, you might see five or six of these lime-kilns burning, little volcanos, the white smoke rising up and drifting along in the breeze. The mothers of the locality, when they saw the smoke, they'd be along to the kiln the following day for an apron-full of the lime; it would be kept in a box below the dresser. Well, a lump of that would be put sizzling in a cup of water, or it might be put steeping in a crock the night before, and every small lad'd have to take a few sups of that before the breakfast. Often I drank it myself . . . it tasted like . . . Oh! . . . the clippings of horse hoofs! But the mothers swore by it, claiming that it killed all the microbes and germs lurking along the 'elementry' canal! You'd want to see no doctor after it; nor was there any living for doctors at that time.

They say the first doctor to come into this corner of the parish was during the 1918 'flu'. He wasn't seen again until the epidemic of appendicitis in the 1930s. Of course, there was the occasional case of the man being sent to Dublin to the specialist. For many of those poor people that trip to Dublin was their first time seeing a train and I don't want to be too hard on the medical profession, but a lot of them went to heaven only seeing the train once!

One night I was at such a venue, the lime-kiln, and a brother's son of my own, Larry, came there for a load of lime, he had the contract of repairing Dr Collins' house — Board of Works job. That very day, he told us, he was putting in a new window, up and down sash, ropes and brass-faced pulleys and so on.

'I had a crock of red lead paint, as specified for the priming,' he said, 'and with whiting and linseed oil, I was making the putty to glaze the sash, when along came Dr Collins. And when he saw the appurtances of my trade he laughed."Aha," he said, "I see putty and paint cover all your mistakes!"

'"That's right, Doctor," I said, "And the spade and shovel cover all yours." He didn't like it at all!'

Medical topics, like talk of love or small potatoes, once the subject comes down there's no knowing where it will end. And that night sitting on a clamp of turf, a few feet

away from the mouth of the volcano, was a Tagney man —
that's a son of his that's married in over there now in Tom
Casey's place. Tagney scrope* the inside of his pipe, a little
smaller than the kiln, and knocking the ashes and bruscar*
of tobaccy into the cover, and putting it on a ciarán* of
turf, he settled himself and said: 'In ancient times in Ireland,
if we can judge by what we hear, if you wanted to go on
for the practice of medicine you wouldn't go to college at
all like now. What'd happen is, you'd serve your time to
the local dispensary man, the same as if you were going in
for tailoring or stone-masoning.

'At that time there was this rich couple and they had no
family only the one son. God help us! as thick as the wall!
The wife thought that it would be a great uplift for 'em in
the community to have the name of having a son a doctor.
And having the money and the influence they got the son
bound down to one Dr Galvin that was operating at the
time. So everywhere the doctor'd go Jack the apprentice'd
be around after him, dressed up to the nines, and a little
hard hat on him.

'They were called out in the country this day where a
man was sick. They went into the kitchen and up in the
room, and Dr Galvin gave the patient a thorough examina-
tion, you may be sure, and put his finger on the complaint
and prescribed for him. When they were going out of the
room Dr Galvin, looking back, said to the patient, "Give up
eating oranges. They don't agree with you constitutionally!"

'Crossing out the yard, Jack the apprentice said to the
doctor, "How in the world did you know the man was
eating oranges?"

'"In our trade," says the doctor, "you must keep your
eyes open. Didn't you see the skins under the bed?"

'That was all right. About a week after, there was
another call, very urgent, and the same day the doctor was
away at a funeral — maybe he had a good right to be
there! And as the call was urgent, Jack said he'd go. Off

with him, with his little bag, into the kitchen bursting with importance and down in the room. He never looked at the patient, no more than I'm looking at the moon this minute, only lifted the quilt and looked under the bed. And there looking out at him was a set of harness! He turned to the patient and with his two thumbs he pushed down the lower eyelids, mercy of God that he didn't blind him with the pressure, and said, "You'll die roaring if you don't give up eating horses!"

'Now that Jack had his first success, according to himself, he decided that he would go off as a journey man — an improver. His father, a saintly man, at the altar every morning, tried to persuade him to wait until he'd have more knowledge, but the mother gave Jack the money to get a doctor's bag and some instruments, a big knife and a saw in case of amputations!

'Jack set out and he was going along but no one put any come hither on him until he met a man of very pale complexion. The pale man asked Jack what his trade was and Jack told him. The pale man said he was fairly well up in medicine himself.

'"Hire me," he said to Jack, "and you won't be sorry!"

'Having a servant, Jack thought, would make him appear more important, so he hired the pale man, and the bargain was that whatever money was made in each case would be divided between 'em. They shook hands on it, and the pale man's hand was as cold as ice.

'It wasn't long until they heard that the son of the richest man in the country was down with some strange malady. His case had bamboozled all medical science, and his father was now offering £500 to any doctor, home or foreign, that could cure his son. Jack and the pale man went up to the house and after explaining who they were, the rich man brought 'em up to the sick room, and there was the son lying on the bed and not a gug* out of him.

'The pale man felt his pulse and told Jack they'd want the sick room to themselves.

'"What do these people want here for?" he said, "they are only using up the air on the sick man. We'll want two pots brought in," he said to Jack, "one with hot water and one with cold."

'This was done, the room was cleared and the patient was now in what is know as intensive care!

'"Where's the doctor's bag?" says the pale man.

'Jack gave it to him. The pale man took out the saw and the knife and like that, in a jiffy, he had the head cut off the patient. He took an herb out of his pocket, the size of a head of caisearbhán,* and rubbed it to the wound above and below, cauterising it. Not a drop of blood flowed. He then took the head by the two ears and ducked it into the hot water, gave it a swirl and then a swee-gee* and like lightning ducked it into the cold skillet. He shook the water off it and landed it back on its place, lined up the wind-pipe, the jugular, the spinal and vocal cords, veins, arteries and blood vessels, gave the head a tap to firm it down, took out some powder, mixed it like pollyfil, and filled the crack all round!

'"Are you all right now?" says the pale man to the patient.

'"I'm fine," says he. "Never felt better in all my life!" And began to dance around.

'The young man's father was delighted, paid the £500, no bother, and Jack and the pale man had to stay the night for a big party, polka sets and everything!

'In the morning, when they got down to the gate of the road, the pale man said to Jack: "What about our bargain? Half the proceeds, wasn't that it?"

'Jack took out the money and lazy enough he was about it too!

'"Ah," says he, "A quarter of it is enough for you, after all I'm the doctor. Your are only the servant."

'The pale man didn't say "yes", "aye" or "no", only turned on his heel and went off, and Jack was left alone. Well, it never rains but it pours. Jack was hardly into the county Limerick when he heard of another young man that was down with the same complaint. His father too was a very rich man, and was offering a reward of £500 to any doctor that could cure his son. Jack went up to the house. The father came out and when Jack told him who he was and the success he had in treating such ailments the father was in the seventh heaven with delight.

'"Come on away in!" he said to Jack.

'But Jack made it plain to him that he would not put his foot inside the threshold, or lay a finger on his son down of £700 — Jack was learning his trade!

'The father agreed; what can you do when your hand is in the dog's mouth.

'Jack went into the house, cleared all the gapers out of the sick room ordered two pots of water, one cold and one hot, took out the knife and the saw and cut the head off the patient. God — all the blood! Then taking the head by the two ears he plunged it into the pot, and when his knuckles met the hot water, he wasn't prepared for it, and damn it if he didn't let the head go. Blessed hour it was like snap-apple night with him trying to retrieve the head, and ages went by before he was able to lever it out with the tongs. Then he plunged it into the cold pot, shook it and put it back in its place, but if the did the head fell one way and the body fell the other. Jack knew now that the devil was done, and he was looking up to see was there a skylight he could get out through. He was shaking with terror and muttering to himself, "Rocks hide me and mountains on me fall!" like sinners will on the last day when they'll see God's face in the heavens.

'With that he heard some commotion outside. It was the pale man trying to get in.

'"Where are you going?" the patient's father wanted to know.

'"I'm the doctor's servant," the pale man said. "He sent me to the apothecary for medicine and I have it here for him."

'He was let in but would he be in time? He took the herb out of his pocket and rubbed it to the head and the body and whatever blood was left in the man was coagulated on the spot. Then he took the head by the two ears. Mercy of God that the ears didn't come away in his hands they were so long in the hot water. Nice and easy he ducked the head into the hot water, gave it a swirl and then a swee-gee,* lifted it out and into the cold water. Another swirl and another swee-gee,* dripped the water off it and landed it back in its place. He had to work like lightning because of the delay. He lined up the wind-pipe, the jugular, spinal and vocal cords, veins, arteries and blood vessels. He was so thorough that he ran his finger under the patient's tongue in case it was curled in his mouth. Then he gave the head a smart tap to firm it down, puttied the crack all round, and said to the patient:

'"Are you all right?"

'"I'm fine!" the patient said, "but awful dizzy!"

'The loss of blood, of course!

'"Plenty of beef tea for the next three weeks running," says Jack, "and you'll be as fit as a fiddle."

'Jack and the pale man ordered a few bags of sawdust to shake on the blood, before they called the father in. When he saw his son able to move around, the father was delighted. He paid the money on the nail, and threw a big dinner for Jack and the pale man.

'When they got down to the gate of the road in the morning, the pale man said: "What about the bargain?"

'"Look," says Jack, "I didn't earn a ha'penny of that money. Take it all, for without you I couldn't cure anyone. I know nothing."

'"That's all I wanted you to admit," says the pale man.

"But money is no good to me where I'm going. Sit down and I'll tell you a story."

They sat down.

'"On the day of my funeral," said the pale man, "my coffin was stopped at the entrance to the graveyard by a man I owed money to. He had a gang with him and they told the mourners that my body wouldn't be buried until my debt was paid. My debts weren't great, but my people were poor and they hadn't that amount of money between them. Now, who should be passing the way but your father, and on hearing the arguing he came up and when he found out what was wrong, he put his hand into his pocket and paid the money, and I got what every man is entitled to, a decent burial."

'"Since you went on the road doctoring, your father has been praying to high heaven for you every morning at the altar. I was in his debt, I couldn't let him down, so that's why I came to save you from the rope! Give me the bag. You can keep the money but let it be the last farthing you'll ever earn at the trade of medicine. If you have to practice, go foreign, and don't be killing Irish people!"'

They went the lower road, I came the high road, they crossed over the stepping stones and I came by the bridge, they were drowned and I was saved and all I ever got for my storytelling was shoes of brown paper and stockings of thick milk. I only know what I heard, I only heard what was said and a lot of what was said was made up to pass the night away!

Glossary

Abhann Uí Chraidha	—	Quagmire river
Abhdhar	—	Amount
Airiú	—	Aroo
Amen, a Thierna	—	Amen, O Lord
Anois	—	Now
Asacán	—	Insult
Balbh	—	Dumb
Banbh	—	Piglet
Bandle	—	A measure of 21 inches, in Irish bannlámh
Bata scóir	—	Tally rod
Bean cabhair	—	help woman
Bí ciúin	—	Be quiet
Bodach	—	Clown
Bonóicín	—	New born infant
Botháns	—	Cabins
Brus	—	Fragments
Bruscar	—	Small pieces (here = dottle)
Cabáiste Scotch	—	Scotch cabbage
Cabúis	—	Cubby-hole
Cadrawling	—	Englicised form of Cadaráil – foolish chatter
Caisearbhán	—	Dandelion
Carn	—	A little heap
Ciarán	—	Small sod of turf
Ciseán	—	Basket
Cliamhain isteach	—	One who marries into a farm

Cnoc an Áir	—	Hill of Slaughter
Cogar i leith, a Cháit	—	Whisper to me, Cáit
Collops	—	Calves
Corp an Diabhail	—	Body of the devil
Corragiob	—	Haunches
Creachaill	—	Gnarled piece of wood
Croí an Diabhail	—	Heart of the devil
Cróitín	—	Byre
Cúilín	—	A nook
Cúl lochta	—	Back loft
Dall Glic	—	Blind expert
Dia linn	—	God be with us
Dia linn is Muire	—	God and Mary be with us
Dia's Muire dhuit	—	God & Mary be with you (Hello)
Diggle	—	Euphemism for devil
Dinger	—	Outstanding thing
Donas	—	Misfortune
Éist	—	Listen
Faill na nGabhar	—	Goat's cliff
Fáilte Romhat	—	Welcome
Figario	—	Unusual item of dress
Fostúch	—	Very large man
Gáirdín na nóinín	—	Garden of daisies
Garsún	—	Young boy
Gimp	—	Urge
Glaise	—	Stream
Golaun	—	Gallán – pillar stone
Gríosach	—	Ashes containing small coals, embers
Grug	—	Haunches
Gug	—	Stir

Lapadawling	—	Lapadáil – Crawling
Laverick	—	Weighty, awkward
Leaca	—	Sloping field
Lipín báite	—	Wet rag
Lop	—	Lapa – Paw
Meas	—	Respect
Mhuire Mháthair	—	Mother Mary
Mothal	—	A bushy head of hair
Nacoss	—	Easy-going
Ootumawling	—	Rummaging
Oright/O'er right	—	Opposite
Padhsán	—	Mean man (complainer)
Páirc a' tSasanaigh	—	Englishman's field
Pillaloo	—	Plague
Pillamiloo	—	Nonsense word
Poltóg	—	A fine walloper of a child
Poursheen	—	Boreen or passageway
Ráiméis	—	nonsense
Sásta	—	Satisfied
Seana	—	Old
Scrope	—	Scraped
Seanchaidhe	—	Storyteller
Skeeting	—	Skating
Slacht	—	Neatness
Smathán	—	A taste, a small measure of whiskey
Smig	—	Chin
Spágs	—	Large, clumsy feet
Sprid an Tobac	—	Tobacco Spirit
Sráthar fhadas	—	Pannier baskets

Stellan	—	Milk-pan stand
Súgán	—	Straw rope
Swee-gee	—	A turn about
Táthaire	—	An impudent fellow
Tóg Bog É	—	Take it easy
Tomhaisín	—	A measure
Trí ráithe	—	Nine months
Tuille	—	A tiley – an added amount
Tulc	—	Lump; overcome with grief
Turtóg	—	A little clump
Welt	—	A blow
Diaidh ar ndiaidh síos le fánaigh (p.12)	—	Little by little with the incline
An rud is annamh is iontach (p.23)	—	What's rare is wonderful
Dá mbead capall ag siúd is istigh cois tine anois a bhínn ag ól té (p.24)	—	If they had a horse it's inside by the fire I'd be now drinking tea
Duirt sí le . . . gan aon Ghaolainn a labairt ós chomhair an tSasanaigh. Bhí go maith agus bhí go holc leis (p.44)	—	She said to . . . not to speak any Irish in front of the Englishman. It was good and bad as well
O mo chircín! Mo chircín, circ! A stór mo chroí istigh. Dia do bheannacha a laog, A leanbhín gleoite (p.45)	—	Oh, my little hen, my heart's treasure. God bless you my beautiful child.

Nach é an trua go deo é go raibh an dinnéar againn (p.46)	Isn't it a terrible pity we had the dinner
Is baolach ná deanfad an gnó (p.47)	I'm afraid I won't do it
Agus do bhí cara mná tí aige an oiche seo in Sráid Bhaisinton (p.48)	And he had a lady friend that night in Washington Street
Idir Clydagh agus Muckross (p.52)	Between Clydagh and Muckross
Trí lár mo chroí tá taithneamh duit (p.52)	In my heart there's affection for you
Go raibh aithne aige ar gharsún mín macánta (p.54)	He knew a fine honest young man
'Ó' ar seisean, 'nach iontach go deo an t-urlabhra an Béarla. D' fhanfainn ag eisteacht leis an gcainnt sin go lá an Luain' (p.55)	'Oh,' says he, 'What a wonderful language English is. I could listen to that talk till doom's day'
Aighneas and Pheacaigh is an Bháis (p.65)	The argument between Death and the Sinner
An Siota is a mháthair (p.65)	The Siota and his mother
Trí mo choir féin, trí mo choir féin, trí mo mhór choir féin (p.67)	Through my fault, through my fault, through my most grevious fault

Bíonn seacht n-insint ar — It is said that there are
gach scéal, a deirtear, agus seven tellings to every
bíodh cluas ghéar againn do story. Let us listen then to
na hinsintí is rogha le duine what the king of the Kerry
de ríscéalaithe Chiarraí (p.72) storyteller has chosen for
us.

Agus gan focal in a phluic — Without a word in his
aige (p.74) mouth

Gruaig ar do cheann, — Hair on your head, light
solus i do shúile agus in your eyes and teeth in
fiachla id' bheal (p.75) your mouth

Feoil agus cnámha ort, cosa — Flesh and bones on you,
agus crúba fút, is earbal legs and hoofs under you
taobh thiar (p.75) and a tail behind

Bhí na cursaí fada go leor — It was a long way for the
ag na spailpíní fadó (p.80) itinerant farm workers
long ago

An puc ar a dhrom aige — Going with his bag on
agus é ag imeacht mar a his back as the old
dúirt na sean daoine (p.80) people said

Tá rud ahmáin cinnte beidh — One thing is sure this
an gleann seo gan táilliúir glen will be without a
(p.105) tailor

Is treise dúchas ná oiliúint — Nature beats training
(p.111)

I AM A YOUNG FELLOW (see page 51)

L2. And the hags of the village wouldn't give me wife or fortune,

L4. And promised the maiden I'd be faithful to her for ever.

L6. And I straightened my horse to meet with my heart's delight.

L8. And we got into Cashel on the morrow at dawn of day.

L10. And oats for the horse and water and plenty of hay.

L12. And she had one hundred and forty fine yellow guineas.

L14. And I sold my horse to the priest of a mountainy parish.

L16 And we left the land with no fear of want or danger.

L18 The tidings were printed in yesterday's *Telegraph News*.

L20. And brought back to Clonmel there to stand our trial.

L22. That I would drink my earnings living an aimless life.

L24: And I slyly deceived her unknown to the world wide.

L26. They enquired from the maiden what was it she had to say.

L28. And she'd marry no other till she was buried beneath the clay.

L30. And we went to the priest to marry my heart's desire.

L32. And we live satisfied with no fear of want or danger.

THE HIRING FAIRS (see page 80)

Never, never again will I go to Cashel
Selling myself and ruining my health there
Sitting by the wall at the side of a street
A slave to be 'bought' at the hiring fair.

Burly landowners coming on horseback
Asking, am I hired to anyone?
Oh I'll hit the road the way is long
'Tis the way of the rambling scythesman.

MORE MERCIER BESTSELLERS

IN MY FATHER'S TIME
Eamon Kelly

In My Father's Time invites us to a night of storytelling by Ireland's greatest and best loved seachaí, Eamon Kelly. The fascinating stories reveal many aspects of Irish life and character. There are tales of country customs; match-making, courting, love; marriage and the dowry system, emigration, American wakes and returned emigrants. The stream of anecdotes never runs dry and the humour sparkles and illuminates the stories.

Nowadays we find it hard to visualise the long dark evenings of times gone by when there was no electric light, radio or television. We find it even harder to realise that such evenings were not long enough for the games, singing, music, dancing and storytelling that went on.

BLESS ME FATHER
Eamon Kelly

Wit, humour and a unique sense of fun abound on every page.

ACCORDING TO CUSTOM — AN EVENING OF STORYTELLING
Eamon Kelly

Not all customs are redolent of evil — many of the customs are humorous and winsome and vouch for the admirable vein in tradition.' (From the Introduction by Bryan MacMahon).

THE RUB OF A RELIC
Eamon Kelly

More tales of country customs from Ireland's greatest contemporary storyteller.

THE BEDSIDE BOOK OF IRISH FOLKLORE
Séamas Ó Catháin

The pages of this book are crammed with colourful folktales and legends, tales of the ghost and fairy world and traditional customs and beliefs which were, and are, an important part of Irish life.

There are riddles and proverbs and tall tales galore. You will also discover cures and remedies for all manner of ailments, from baldness and drunkenness, and even advice on love potions.

These stories, gathered from the four corners of Ireland, are told in the original words of the storytellers of old and make lively and exciting reading.

FOLKTALES OF THE IRISH COUNTRYSIDE
Kevin Danaher

In this heartwarming collection of tales that spring naturally from the Irish countryside, Kevin Danaher remembers some forty stories told to him long ago when country folk entertained themselves of an evening with singing, dancing and storytelling. Some are stories told by members of his own family; others he took down in his own countryside from the last of the great traditional *seanchaí*. Included are tales of giants and ghosts, of wondrous deeds and queer happenings, of fairies and kings, beautiful princesses and wicked mischief-makers.

SUPERSTITIONS OF THE IRISH COUNTRY PEOPLE
Padraic O'Farrell

Do you know why it is considered unlucky to meet a barefooted man, to start out on a journey on the tenth of November, to get married on a Saturday?

Irish country people believe that angels are always present amoung them and that all good things — crops, rain and so forth come from them. Bad spirits bring sickness to humans, animals and pestilence to crops. They do not speak of fairies on Wednesdays or Fridays for on those days they could be present while still being invisible.

Living, it its fullest sense is still dear to the Irish country folk and is reflected in their customs. In the countryside life still has dignity and people are not mere statistics. Going to work, to sea, to weddings, wakes — at all of these there are fascinating customs to be observed.

The Tailor and Ansty
Eric Cross

'Tis a funny state of affairs when you think of it.' It is
the Tailor himself speaking. 'The book is nothing but
the fun and the talk and the laughter which has gone on
for years around this fireside . . .'

The Tailor and Ansty was banned soon after its first
publication in 1942 and was the subject of such bitter
controversy that it may well have influenced the later relaxation
of the censorship law. Certainly it has become a modern Irish
classic, promising to make immortals of the Tailor and his
irrepressible foil, his wife, Ansty, and securing a niche in Irish
letters for their Boswell, Eric Cross.

The Tailor never traveller further than Scotland and yet
the width of the world can hardly contain his wealth of humour
and fantasy. Marriages, inquests, matchmaking, wakes –
everything is here. Let the Tailor round it off with a verse of a
ballad:

Now all you young maidens,
Don't listen to me
For I will incite you to immoralitee,
Or unnatural vice or in a similar way
Corrupt or deprave or deprave you or lead you astray.

Stories from the Tailor
Edited and Translated by Aindrias Ó Muimhneacháin

Frank O'Connor in his introduction to *The Tailor and Ansty* said:

> Neighbours, visitors and students would pause for a
> chat with him, students because he spoke beautiful
> Irish, visitors because they found his English
> conversations entertaining enough. It was, though it
> was not as good as his Irish conversation. In Irish he
> had a whole field of folk stories and songs to fall back
> on...

Aindrias Ó Muimhneacháin has edited and translated these
wonderful stories and they are now available for the first time in
English.

The Tailor was a remarkable storyteller and he had his own
special way of telling stories. In *Stories from the Tailor* we hear
him talk and we enter into another world as we listen to tales of
charms, superstitions, spirits, pookas, the Good People, diseases
and traditional cures. We see his humour and laughter and his
extraordinary spirit shines through all his stories.